CHRISTINE OF THE FOURTH

"You think you have the right to run everyone's lives,"
flushed Christine.

CHRISTINE
OF THE FOURTH

by
W. E. EASTWAYS

TO

My Brothers

CONTENTS

CONTENTS

CHAPTER ONE

SHEILA RETURNS TO GREYCOURT

Sheila Conway ran up the staircase in pleasurable excitement, pausing half-way up to give a contented sniff at her surroundings. Oh, it was good to be back at old Greycourt after a whole year's absence; good to see again its quaint nooks and crannies; to feel the absolute quiet that prevailed about this time of day. She hummed a little tune under her breath, as she ran up the next few stairs. Quiet—that was the keynote here, it—

Crash! The Fourth Common Room door opened and Sheila jumped back as a girl came hurtling through the doorway, to land almost at her feet. Sheila bent over to help her up, but the girl struck her hand aside, and scrambling up made off down the corridor. Sheila gazed after her in shocked surprise for a moment, then opened the door of the common room. There was a threatening surge of Fourth Formers towards her—then suddenly a shout.

"Sheila!"

And in an instant, all her old friends were around, vociferous with welcomes.

"It's good to see you again, Shee."

"How was that awful school in the back of beyond?"

"How's your sister now?"

"Oh, I'm glad you're back for the Fourth, Sheila, old girl!"

They pushed her into a chair, and grouped themselves around, clamouring for news. Yes, they were all there, just as she had pictured them many a time. Red-haired Ronnee Parnell, wistful dark-eyed Maureen Linney, Connie Forman, the captain, and all the others—a little more grown up, otherwise just the same. But were they the same?

"It's wonderful to be back," she declared. "I've looked forward to this all the time I've been away. But—wait, I'll tell you about everything in a minute, but do tell me this. Was that girl thrown out just now, or did I—?"

"She *was* thrown out," Ronnee informed her shortly.

"But, but—"

"But me no buts," quoted Sally Haines. "She's the bane of our existence, the pest of the Fourth. She's a terrible nuisance, and we don't want to talk about her. Tell us your news, there's a sweet child."

Sheila turned bewildered, to Connie. "Look,

just tell me this, and I'll stop asking questions—
What has she done?"

Connie looked as if the subject were very
distasteful to her. "Well," she said unwillingly,
"I suppose you'd better know about it, but we're
very tired of her, I can tell you. And it isn't as
if," added Connie, "we haven't done all we can
for her, because we have."

"I'm glad to hear it," Sheila said seriously. "I
don't mind telling you that I never expected to
see *that*," jerking her head towards the door,
"happen at Greycourt."

Connie was impatient at the interruption.
"Nor would we. Anyway, this is what happened.
She came here last year with such a sad story
that we all made a frightful fuss of her. The
Sixth, and the Mistresses as well, used to pet her,
and I must say we all liked her very much. She
was quick and witty, pretty good at games,
especially tennis, and I suppose we all lost our
heads about her."

"Until she started showing off," put in Valerie
Kingshead.

"Yes, for some unknown reason she suddenly
became unbearable; conceited wasn't the word for
it. She'd dictate to everybody, and mimic horridly
—oh, I can't tell you all she did, but she had
everybody's back up in the end."

Sheila was frowning thoughtfully. "It's not
for me to say," she began, "but couldn't you

just have left her alone completely until—"

"No, it's not for you to say," broke in Ronnee hotly, "you weren't here. We tried ignoring her; we tried being rude to her; in fact we tried everything we knew, but it was no good. How would *you* like a bottle of ink deliberately tipped over an exercise you'd just finished? How would *you* like to find the dog dressed up in your best blouse? Would *you* be pleased if you found a squashed tomato in the toe of your shoe? Yes," Ronnee relaxed suddenly with a grin, for all the others were laughing, "it sounds funny now, but *we* got into a row each time. She didn't. Old Janet, who makes out she's hot at psychology says that Christine is determined to be in the limelight, by fair means or foul. Well, she's never out of the limelight, and we're fed to the teeth with her."

"Well, that's old Ronnee for you," the Captain chuckled. "Now you've heard all about it. You tell us your news."

Sheila didn't feel at all satisfied that she had heard all about it, but she complied with their request and told them about the year she had spent in the Isle of Wight. She and her family had lived with friends there, during her sister's convalescence from illness, and Sheila had gone to a day school. She had enjoyed life on the whole, but had longed all the time to get back.

"Well, now you're back, it's much the same as

ever. Oh, we have our pocket money taken away for untidiness and so forth, instead of conduct marks. That's one change."

That wouldn't worry Sheila much. As far as pocket money went, she was one of the lucky ones; but it did worry quite a few of the Fourth Formers.

But the Fourth were still fussing round their newly-restored friend. "Come and look around," urged Sally and Sheila was only too glad to comply with her request. There was the usual grand display of books, many of them left behind by former Fourth girls, for the Fourth at Greycourt had acquired a reputation for literature, and each successive generation tried to live up to it.

"Did you have a library at that frightful school?" inquired Janet, with conscious Greycourt superiority.

"It wasn't a frightful school," defended Sheila instantly. "I liked it there, but it wasn't Greycourt. You'll hardly believe me when I tell you that the girls there were rather sorry for me because I was at an old school like this. I soon put them right there, of course."

"Should think so indeed!" Connie snorted. She held Sheila's thick plait of hair admiringly. "Still got your long mop I see. Oh, by the way, here's something new." She indicated a tall fair girl who was sitting in the background, smiling as if the whole proceedings amused her very much. "This is Priscilla Westerham. Quite new; we've only just unpacked for her."

"Something indeed!" echoed the new girl with mock indignation. She came forward to shake hands with Sheila. "The only packing they were interested in was my box of eatables. Still—" she grinned suddenly, displaying two rows of perfect teeth, "I've already heard quite a bit about you, Sheila, and I'm glad to know you."

"That's nice, thanks." Sheila liked the look of the new girl and showed that she did. She slipped her hand through Priscilla's arm. "Come and inspect with me. By the way, do you do anything?"

Priscilla hesitated. "I'm not very good at games, if that's what you mean, but—"

"She plays the piano though," interrupted Maureen, "and are we going to make use of her!" Maureen knew all the latest dances, and taught the other girls, but they usually had to wait for someone to play the piano in the school hall. No one hitherto had shone in the musical direction in the Fourth.

Connie once again took up the rôle of guide. "Lina Short's mother sent us the cushions and the tablecloth. Wasn't it kind of her? You didn't know Lina. She was only here a year— very delicate. Oh, see this nearly empty bookcase?

Well, one of the school patrons, who has a soft spot for the Fourth, provided a fund for a book each month that the Fourth came up to a decent average in work and conduct. And if any girl was outstanding, she was to get a book as well. I can't see the Fourth doing it."

Up went Sheila's head, "Why ever not?"

"Christine—that's why ever not," Maureen supplied the information with a humorous lilt in her pretty voice. "She'll see that we stay at the bottom in everything. She did last term in the Third. Nobody thinks anything of us because of her."

"Which reminds me," exclaimed Sheila, and they all groaned. "Why were you all so sorry for her when she came?"

"Here it comes girls!" Connie gave in with a laugh. "Our Sheila doesn't change much, does she? Well, here's what happened. She came here as an ordinary new girl and we'd never have known otherwise if she hadn't told her story herself. It seemed that her father was in prison— yes, prison," as Sheila exclaimed. "We were too petrified to ask why, of course, but we think he was a Bank Manager and something went wrong with the accounts. Christine insisted that he was the victim of circumstances. She wasn't a bit ashamed about it, and we all rather admired her."

"Sure and aren't all the best people in prison nowadays," put in Maureen wickedly.

"My mother nearly had a fit," said Janet. "She said at first she'd take me away, but the matter dropped. I believe someone who approached Merry on the subject was snubbed pretty badly."

"Anyway," continued Connie, "she told us quite simply all that had happened to her. Her mother, who was an invalid, died from shock, and it seemed as if they hadn't got any friends or relations, because none turned up."

"It's a habit they have when there's trouble," said Janet, the gloomy one.

Sheila shivered, "Don't talk like that, Janet!" she begged. "Go on, Connie."

"I don't know that there's much more to tell. They had a couple of servants, and one of them took Christine to her home until something could be arranged. There's a welfare centre there as it happens, and an old Greycourtier who visited there got interested and managed to have Christine sent here."

"How lovely of her! It sounds like a book," cried Sheila, her eyes shining. "Christine must have been relieved."

"That's just what she wasn't," Ronnee said in her emphatic way. "She'd got fond of the slum people by then, and she only came here as a favour to Mrs. Cameron. Now, of course, she pretends she is dying to get back to the slum."

There was a general laugh, and when Sheila

looked around for the cause, Connie explained. "It isn't a slum really. I believe it's quite a decent part of London, but her friends are poor, and their house is rather crowded as it is."

"Look, there she goes!" exclaimed Ronnee, who was standing at the window. Sheila ran over, and was just in time to see Christine disappear through a doorway.

"Why—isn't that the—er domestic quarters?" she asked, surprised.

"That is," Maureen assured her solemnly, "ze kitcheen, as ever was. She has friends there. Mrs. Cameron, who never does things by halves —she's American, perhaps that accounts for it— got her slum acquaintance a job as assistant cook. Friend Christine has been on the carpet once or twice for going there, but I expect she's more of a trial to Miss Meredith than she is to us. You see, she *wants* to be expelled."

But now Sheila slipped hurriedly over to the door before the girls could stop her. "See you later," she said and closed the door behind her.

"Hey! Where are you off to, Sheila?" called out Maureen, feeling that her story had been interrupted.

"Can't you guess?" Connie said resignedly.

They could. Sheila had a reputation for getting the best out of other people, and she was off to try her hand on Christine. They all laughed.

"Here's wishing her luck," grinned Ronnee.

CHAPTER TWO

GETTING ACQUAINTED

Sheila found, however, that it wasn't going to be so easy to find Christine. That young lady had vanished from sight and Sheila was accorded a very cold welcome in the kitchen.

"Now then, Missie, you've no business to be here," exclaimed the cook, bustling forward and looking angry. "You know the rule—why—!" she broke off, her face lighting up with a smile. "Why, it's Miss Sheila, isn't it? Well I never!"

"I'm glad you remember me," Sheila laughed as she shook hands. "I won't keep you a minute, but do just tell me where Christine is."

The cook looked troubled. "I don't know, my dear, and that's the truth. She's not here now, and I wish she—I mean I wish none of you would come here."

"All right, Mrs. Marsden, don't you worry," Sheila said reassuringly, "I'll go. I—I suppose you couldn't give me a hint?"

"You didn't meet her, did you?" Cook was actually smiling.

'No, I didn't."

"Well, she couldn't have gone *that* way then."

"Thanks for the tip," laughed Sheila, and went out to walk in the opposite direction from which she had come, but there was no sign of Christine. Sheila looked from left to right, and went down one or two garden paths, unaware that Christine Barry was watching here with amusement from the branches of a tree. That lady had coaxed a cake and an apple from the cook, had picked up a picture paper without troubling anyone for permission and had settled herself quite comfortably in her usual retreat. The fact that it was strictly forbidden to visit the kitchen, or to eat at any but the authorised time, did not worry her at all. She leaned forward to watch this search for herself for she had guessed, as soon as she saw Sheila, that she was in for another dose of being reformed. Several people had tried their hand at it and retired baffled.

And now Sheila had disappeared. Surely she hadn't given up already! Christine leaned forward at a perilous angle and the newspaper slipped to the ground. She drew back quickly in annoyance but Sheila had seen her.

"Hallo!" she called out coolly, as if it were the most natural thing in the world to find someone up in a tree in a deserted part of the grounds.

Christine did not answer but just stared back at her.

"I'm Sheila Conway," continued Sheila cheerily.

"I used to be here, but the whole family moved to the Isle of Wight because of my sister; she was ill, you know. You're Christine Barry, they tell me. Are you called Chris?"

"Only by my friends," returned the girl in the tree crisply. She jumped down and began to walk away. Sheila immediately fell into step beside her.

"Mind if I come along?" she asked.

Christine shrugged. "It's not my school. You can go where you like."

But Sheila only laughed. She was so unused to this sort of treatment that it intrigued her, and it was the other girl who first broke the silence as they made their way out of the gardens and into the field.

"I suppose you've been hearing of all my dreadful carryings-on," she remarked scornfully.

"Yes, I've been hearing about you," Sheila said candidly. "Not all about you, I guess," she added, her eyes twinkling, "there hasn't been time."

Christine surveyed her with something like curiosity behind her antagonism. "Corkscrews!" she exclaimed softly, as if to herself, "I believe there's a sense of humour here somewhere." Then she looked Sheila up and down insolently. "Are you going to try to make me a model schoolgirl? Of course, I couldn't aspire to be a model Greycourt girl."

"Poor old Greycourt, she can take it." Sheila

smiled, though the colour mounted to her cheeks, for no Greycourtier takes kindly to disparagement of her school. "Would you like to be a model schoolgirl?" she asked sweetly.

"*No, thank you!*" the other replied explosively; then she laughed.

Sheila laughed too. "Come on, let's go to tea," she said coaxingly. "You don't know what a thrill it is for me to be back. I'm even longing to see the school at tables in the dining hall"

"You don't know what a thrill it would be for me to leave."

But Sheila would not be drawn into an argument. "Never satisfied, are we?" she remarked cheerfully. "Come on."

Christine sighed in an exasperated fashion. "There seems to be no getting rid of you. But don't imagine I shall always come with you. It just suits me now, that's all."

"Don't imagine I shall always want you with me," returned Sheila calmly, and at that, Christine laughed again. She appreciated this sort of behaviour. It didn't savour of reform. The two walked together to dining hall, where they met the rest of the form.

"Come up here, Sheila," called out Connie softly. "Tell us about the other school."

"What, here?" Sheila looked astonished.

"Yes. We can talk as we like now at tea-time. Miss Meredith asked us what privileges we'd like in honour of Peace and we chose this. It used to be such a fag to talk in French. Of course, the Sixth still do. We can sit where we like, too."

"Oh, nice!" Sheila dragged the unwilling Christine down beside her, before she had a chance to protest. The girls glanced at each other. They weren't at all pleased to have the "pest" among them, but Sheila refused to notice their disapproval, and told her story gaily. Towards the end of tea-time, Margaret Rainer, the head girl, came down from her table next to Great and greeted Sheila warmly.

"It's good to have you back at Greycourt." She shook hands as she spoke. "How's your hockey?"

"Middling, Margaret. I haven't played a lot."

"Never mind; get in as much practice as you can. We've a grand new coach. She'll get you on."

"Hockey—kids' game!" sneered Christine.

Sheila waited, horror-stricken, for the Captain to wither this presumptuous Fourth Former, but to her amazement, Margaret took no notice whatever of her, and entered into a discussion with the other girls at the table. She was a busy person, however, and a glance at the clock made her rise hurriedly.

"I must run. Do your best, and I'll help as much as I can."

They smiled gratefully at her as she made her

way down the long room, in the poised manner which seemed to come naturally to Greycourt captains. She was always friendly to them.

"Fancy, she was in the Fourth when I last remember her," mused Sheila.

"Well, she ought to sympathise with our woes then," laughed Maureen. "The dear knows we have enough to—"

But at this point, Christine broke in.

"Chat–chat–chat–chat–chat!" she jeered. "Talk about the parrot house at the Zoo!"

The silence that followed was so pointed, that Sheila, feeling guilty, got up quickly and took Christine away.

CHAPTER THREE

AN INVITATION

School settled quickly down into routine and a week had slipped away. Sheila found it easier to pick up the threads than she had expected and soon fell into her old place in the form. Contrary to expectations, Christine seemed as if she were going to behave herself. In any case, Sheila had made up her mind to befriend her, and the Fourth knew of old that when Sheila made up her mind there was no moving her.

"Never mind. Wait till the valiant Christine blows up," prophesied Connie. "That'll shake her!"

And the others chuckled. It wasn't that they were particularly anxious to see Christine "blow up", but Sheila had made it rather obvious that she thought they had been unjust to a girl less fortunate than themselves. Another week passed well on its way, however, without any trouble and the Fourth began to hope that this would be a peaceful term, though it seemed almost too much to hope for.

Priscilla Westerham proved to be a great acquisition. She would sit at the piano in their common room, for as long as they liked and play everything they asked. She had a real gift for singing simple little songs too, and in between she would improvise softly in a very soothing manner.

Margaret, the head girl, came in hurriedly one day but paused at the sight of the group of girls around the piano.

"Well, this is nice!" she exclaimed in pleased surprise. "What a treat to find anyone who will play the piano willingly. You'll be in great demand here, Priscilla."

Priscilla was smiling shyly, when Christine burst into a scornful laugh. "You'll be in great demand, Priscilla," she mimicked, "that is, until a new sensation comes along."

Sheila held her breath with horror, but Margaret said pleasantly:

"Priscilla will find out for herself if that is the truth. And you, Christine," she continued just as pleasantly, "will write out fifty times 'I must not be rude.'"

"I won't!"

"Sixty times. If you haven't written it out and brought it to me by six-thirty, I shall make an appointment for you with Miss Meredith. And now, girls," Margaret's firm lips curved into a smile, "I've come to ask for something. I'm always begging, aren't I? Although I know you are busy making things for the bazaar, I want you to help me too, to make some money this term, so that we can give our men a splendiferous time at Christmas. Give little concerts, and give a few coppers each week from your pocket money. It'll soon add up. They're always so glad to see us, and goodness knows they deserve any little thing that we can do for them."

"Oh yes, Margaret," chorused the Fourth enthusiastically. The soldiers in the hospital a little way out of the village of Greatoaks had been adopted with pride by the Greycourt girls, who on several occasions had gone over to the pleasant hospital to entertain them.

Margaret glanced at the clock and jumped up.

"The prefects are waiting for me. I must go. Oh!" she turned back suddenly. "Just one thing. Hockey. We cut a very poor figure last year. Yes, I know there was quite a bit of illness, and several sprained ankles and no Coach, but we haven't those excuses this year. I absolutely forbid any of you to sprain your ankles. Hockey with a capital 'H' it is, and Hilda has promised to round you up for me."

The Fourth groaned. Hilda Cartip, vice-captain, was a very fussy person and they all fought shy of her. Rather than have her fussing round them like an old hen, they would be down to practise and Margaret knew it. She departed laughing.

"I say, it's a smashing idea about giving concerts," Maureen declared excitedly. "We can do something good now that Priscilla's here to accompany us."

"And I'll dig out my cine-projection," offered Ronnee Parnell. "The films aren't frightfully new, but no one here has seen them yet. We can charge tuppence a show—this room will do for it."

"Oh, fine!" and the girls continued to discuss the various ways in which they could make money. Sheila looked across at Christine once or twice rather uncertainly, but that damsel was sitting in the most comfortable chair and reading. At length, under cover of the general conversation, Sheila made her way over to Christine. But she had already found that it wasn't easy to tackle her in the right way, and she hesitated now as to what course she should take.

"You know, Christine, you really should be getting on with your imposition," announced Christine herself, with her eyes still upon the book she was reading. Then she looked up suddenly, "Isn't that what you are trying to say?" she demanded.

Sheila covered her confusion with a laugh. "Yes, you little wretch," she said. "I was going to say just that."

"Come on then," said Christine unexpectedly. "I'll do it if you'll come too."

"Of course I'll come." Sheila was delighted at this change in her friend. "Margaret really is a dear. I'm so glad."

"Oh, I'm not doing it for *her*," Christine declared derisively, "but she might keep her threat about Miss Meredith, and I don't see why I should be badgered by the Head, too."

Sheila kept silent, though she was bursting to argue the matter with this wilful girl. They went into the Form room together, and Sheila read while Christine sat at her desk and wrote. The imposition did not take long, and after it was delivered to the Captain's room Christine was inclined to be talkative.

"That new girl—Priscilla What's-her-name, is quite good, up to a point, isn't she?"

"She's very good without any point."

"Well, you can go back to the Com. Room if you like."

"Yes, I know."

Christine laughed again in her unexpected way. "You simply are *not* going to argue, are you?" she asked, looking with bright questioning eyes at her companion. "If I'm to be reformed, you have to hold back all you'd like to say. I'm right, aren't I?"

Sheila shook her head helplessly. "You're uncanny," she answered. "I don't know how you think these things. But you're not going to put me off my stroke," she added firmly.

"And you don't want to go back to Priscilla?"

"Oh, I wouldn't say that. She's rather nice."

And at that, and because they were school-girls, they both burst out laughing. They walked along in amiable silence until they reached the small study hall near their classroom.

"What's so wonderful about her?" Christine asked at last.

"I didn't say she was wonderful. But—well, she plays beautifully, you know."

"That's nothing." Christine waved her hand. "If you are so fond of music—well, I sing a bit."

"Do you? I'd like to hear."

The other girl looked about her, then opened the lid of the cabinet gramophone which stood in the room. She picked up a record and looked at it. "I know this one," and without more ado she set it in motion. In a few moments she was singing effortlessly, and piercing sweet like a boy, and she was gratified at the rapt look on Sheila's face as she switched off the recording at the end of her song.

"Like it?" she asked casually.

"It was lovely," breathed Sheila. "I'd no idea. Christine, you *must* sing more than—"

"Come on!" Christine urged, as if the praise upset her.

Sheila only laughed, and they went along the corridor to their form room. They were a little early, after all, for prep., and as they sat waiting

Sheila said quietly, "I want you to come home with me for Christmas."

"W-what!"

"Yes, I do. We could have a good time. I'll ask Mother to send you an invitation. You needn't be alarmed. We all bring our friends home with us."

But for once, Christine was so dumbfounded that all she could say was, "Er—thank you."

CHAPTER FOUR

PREPARING FOR THE PAGEANT

"Fun and Games," announced Maureen, as she joined her friends at hockey practice. "We're going to have a pageant."

"Pageant? What sort of pageant?"

"There's only one sort of pageant," said Maureen, with a wealth of pity in her voice. "A pageanty pageant—you know—all pageant."

"She must mean a *pageant* girls," Ronnee Parnell said softly.

"Cut out the cleverness," begged Connie. "What's it all about, Maureen?"

Maureen shook her head. "I've only heard that Miss Meredith is going to speak to us all, this evening, about a pageant that's to come off soon. Something to do with the Centenary celebrations."

"Oh, smashing! I wondered what we'd be doing about the Centenary business. Wonder who'll be in it?"

"I wonder if I could prevail upon you to get on with practice," Sheila put in patiently.

"There's only a quarter of an hour left."

"Oh, Sheila, have a heart!" pleaded Valerie. "We only have a centenary once every hundred years. Hockey's any old time."

"Off you go!" was Sheila's response to this and, groaning, the girls got back into position. The quarter of an hour soon went by however, and they were free to chatter at tea-time about the forthcoming celebrations. And later, Miss Meredith, who had a way of taking the school into her confidence, spoke to the girls quite freely.

"I think if we all work hard," she began informally, "we shall have time to produce a play-pageant for the Greycourt Centenary, in addition to the originally planned concert. It has been written by an old Courtier—Joan Winter—and embodies the very spirit of this ancient foundation. Miss Dyson will take charge of the arrangements and I want you to give her all the help you can. Miss Dyson will come to each form in turn to choose suitable girls for the parts. That is all, girls."

She looked around smiling, and Margaret rose hurriedly to her feet and wished the headmistress good night on behalf of the school. Great excitement prevailed following this announcement, for it was to be entertainment out of the usual rut.

"I wonder if any of us will be in it!" mused Connie. "It would be nice."

"You'd do for a row of stuffed dummies," Christine told them in her rudest tones. "As petrified codfish perhaps with mouths agape. Dear me, aren't you all noble and forbearing to-day!" she continued, as they disdained to answer. "Did you know, Sheila, that these same noble people heaved me out of the room the other day? Oh, yes, of course you were there. I suppose there will be nothing of that in the pageant?"

Sheila did not answer.

"Do you know, Sheila," Ronnee said in the same tone," that for a whole year we've tried to do what we were taught to do in the First Form—not let past Courtiers down. It was all wasted though. I suppose if a person's impossible, she's just impossible and that's all there is about it. It's a pity she ever came here, and I don't think Greycourt will notice it when she goes."

The others nodded vigorous agreement, though Christine smiled derisively. Sheila still made no answer, and presently, as the conversation became general, she and Christine slipped out of the room. Immediately, Maureen walked over to a mirror and began to make the most astounding grimaces.

"What on *earth*—!" began Connie.

"Petrified codfish," explained Maureen. "I can't get the mouth right. I haven't enough lip."

"You've got too much lip," Ronnee told her, laughing.

"Ugh! That sounds like Christine," shuddered Maureen. "And yet she's funny, isn't she girls? If only her fun weren't so horribly rude!"

"And in the meantime, Sheila might as well be back in the Isle of Wight. How on earth can she stand the creature?"

"Wait till she's had her as long as we have. Anyway, don't let's bother about her now. Turn on the wireless, old thing," and the Fourth settled down philosophically to enjoy itself in its own way.

The next afternoon they had another visitor to their common room, Miss Dyson, the senior music mistress. She was looking very business-like and evidently had no time to waste.

"Now, girls," she said briskly, "I want some of you for the pageant. First of all, girls with long hair. You, Connie, Sheila, Janet. Priscilla, you play the piano—over here, please. Now singers. You won't be seen by the way, but you'll have a lot to do. You'll be a speaking chorus in the beginning and an angels' chorus at the end, and an explanation chorus the rest of the time. Which of you sings? I shall of course have to try out your voices."

"Ronnee and Valerie," volunteered the girls.

"Right. Anyone else?"

"Maureen is a good alto," suggested Sally Haines.

"Good. Will you three stand with the others?"

Miss Dyson was folding up her papers when Sheila, who had been nerving herself for the effort, ventured to say, "Christine sings nicely too."

There was just a shade of hesitation before Miss Dyson answered, "Thank you, Sheila. Christine, go with the others."

For one moment, Christine was so flabbergasted that she almost refused, but the look of disapproval on the faces of the Fourth made up her mind for her. Anything to annoy them! She walked jauntily over to the chosen group.

"Will you girls go to the small study hall and wait for me, please. I have a few more selections to make," and Miss Dyson hurried off to the Lower Fourth.

"Phew! That was quick work!" exclaimed Maureen.

"I'm glad I'm behind the scenes," Ronnee added. "I'm able to see the show, and not have to act myself."

Christine was looking sulky, and Sheila wondered if she had been wise in pushing her forward. There was no opportunity for recriminations, for a number of Sixth Formers as well as Fifth Formers had gathered in the study hall, and at Greycourt one kept silent in august company such as this. Soon Miss Dyson returned, bringing several more girls with her, and the real business of the afternoon began. Parts were distributed and voices tried out. The older girls had the most important parts of course, but there were many lesser characters to be portrayed. Miss Dyson gave them a general outline of the pageant, which would depict certain of the more famous scenes of Greycourt history.

"As well as being word perfect in your parts, get right into the atmosphere of the story," Miss Dyson told them. "Get so much into the spirit of it, that you will feel like a Greycourtier of hundreds of years ago, not just a present day one. Be interested enough to read up about the customs of old Greycourt. Do let us have a really historical and moving pageant. Priscilla, I shall require you for all practices, and perhaps even on the night. Margaret, will you take over please. I want all those with speaking or acting parts to be in this room at three o'clock to-morrow, to run over the lines."

Miss Dyson left them and for a few moments they remained in the study hall. The older girls were quite friendly.

"Well, I hope we'll do old Greycourt proud," Jane Dawe of the Sixth said, with a grin. "It's rather fun to think that we're the ones doing it this time. Wonder what sort of people did it a hundred years ago?"

"Oh, don't be gruesome, Jane."

But lovely Monica Newell said dreamily, "Yes, that's what we have to visualise—what sort of people were here a hundred years ago. It's going to be interesting."

"Time to go, everybody! To-morrow at three o'clock!" called out Margaret, and she waited with her hand on the light switch until the hall was empty.

Sheila turned, a little apprehensively to Christine, as they walked back with the other Fourth Formers, but Christine was looking strangely happy.

"I *am* glad you proposed me, Sheila," she said. "I like all this sort of thing."

"I'm glad too," was all that Sheila replied, but her heart lightened, and she was convinced that a step in the right direction had been taken that afternoon.

CHAPTER FIVE

PRISCILLA'S TURN

"The Cycling Club will reassemble in the Green Court on Saturday week at 2 p.m. Destination Maidens Hill. All intending to come must let me know by Monday at the latest so that arrangements may be made for tea. Outstanding subscriptions should, if possible, be paid before the run.

"MARGARET RAINER,
"Captain."

"Whee! That's wonderful!" exulted Maureen to the group of Fourth Formers looking up at the notice board. "I hoped it would start up again this term and I've brought my bike back."

"So did I," Ronnee said, and, "So did I," said several other girls.

"Of course, we're in the Senior School now," Sheila exclaimed. "Oh dear. I'll write home to Mother; she'll let me have hers I know. I can't possibly ask for a new one now. Still, I'm as tall as Mother. Exciting!"

"Maidens Hill—a bit of a climb," objected Janet.

"Yes, but think of the view, and tea up there too! It'll be good to get some air into our lungs," Sheila paused in her enthusiasm. "What about you, Christine?"

Christine shook her head at once.

"Look, I'll ask for my sister's bicycle as well," Sheila said persuasively. "You're about the same height, and she mustn't ride for a long time. I'm sure she won't mind."

"Well, no if you don't mind," Christine began, "I really—"

"Christine has a brand new bike of her own," Maureen broke in crisply.

"It isn't mine," Christine retorted angrily, but Maureen looked scornful.

"Who *did* Mrs. Cameron buy it for then? I don't remember her asking anyone else if they'd like a new bike."

But, as usual, Sheila poured oil on the troubled waters. "Well, never mind, as long as you've got a bicycle," she told Christine. "I'm longing to show you some of lovely old Sussex."

Christine accepted the inevitable with a shrug. Already she was beginning to realise that for all her gentle ways, Sheila usually carried the day in an argument and quite frankly, as long as it annoyed the rest of the form, Christine had no objections to Sheila's efforts on her behalf.

"Shure, and here's another notice by word of mouth," called out Maureen as the girls began to disperse. "This evening, as ever was, there will be a grand entertainment in the small study hall. Cinema, no less, mark you. Ronnee's, of course."

"Truly, Ronnee?" The girls came crowding back. "Tell us—what films?"

Ronnee giggled. "We-ell, they won't be very up to date I'm afraid—in fact, they'll be most unusual, but I'll show you what I've got. Priscilla will play an opening piece, and we'll put on a record half-way through and all the lot will only cost you tuppence each towards the fund. Mind you all turn up, and bring anyone else who'll come."

"Oh, we'll come!" they promised for, in school, anything out of the ordinary is an event. And they turned up in force after tea, with as many recruits as they could muster. Margaret, who came upon them by chance was prevailed upon to become the guest of honour, though she stifled a sigh at the thought of missing an hour's quiet study. Maureen stood at the door collecting the entrance fees, and dealt severely with any persons who tried to slip in without payment. When it was evident that no more audience was to be expected, Maureen closed the door and stood with her back against it; no one should enter unlawfully if she could help it!

Meanwhile, Ronnee was adjusting her cine-projector and trying to put her films into some sort of order, but the remarks all around confused her, and she signalled desperately to Priscilla to open the proceedings.

"Be quiet, all of you!" she called out. "'Cilla's going to play."

There were loud cheers as Priscilla, with a smile, ran her fingers over the keys. Then she began to play simple well-known airs, and soon the girls were singing in unison. This proved to be so popular that it began to seem to Ronnee as if the entertainment were changing its nature.

"Hi!" she bawled out over the din, "this is supposed to be a film show, not a musical recital. That's enough singing."

"Well, get on with the show then," called back the audience.

"Put the lights out, Maureen," directed Ronnee, and the show began. The first effort called forth howls of derision, for the picture appeared upside down. Ronnee grinned.

"Wait a minute; don't be so impatient." And she readjusted the film. The girls were ready to be amused and laughed uproariously at the ancient Mickey Mouse picture, until it broke down, when they cheered ironically. Ronnee began to get rather flurried.

"Wait a minute," she said again, "I'll put another one in."

But the next film, a still more ancient one, broke down almost as quickly, and once more pandemonium broke out.

"Give us our tuppences back!"

"What a terrible old camera! Where did you get it? Jumble Sale?"

Maureen switched on the lights suddenly, as an idea came to her.

"Ladies and Otherwise!" she called through the din, "I have an announcement to make." And when the noise had subsided she continued: "For the good of the Cause, we are going to charge an extra halfpenny every time the film goes through without breaking down."

There was a moment's silence and then a roar of laughter, so loud and sustained that Margaret had to ask them to subdue their mirth, though she too was laughing. It was just like Maureen to think a way out of an awkward situation like this. But for the remainder of the film entertainment the girls sat up expectantly, applauding every time the show broke down, groaning when the picture ran its course normally. By the end of the evening they each owed three half-pence to the fund, but they were so tickled with the idea that they did not begrudge it, especially as Margaret was there to receive their contributions.

"Thanks very much Fourth," she said, chuckling, "I still think you've been forced into the extra generosity, but as you don't mind, why should I?" And she left them to wind up with a dance. Even Christine was laughing as they left the study hall later. Sheila was beginning to breathe more easily about her friend, for Christine had not been rude to anyone for several days. Of course they were busy days, the pageant was beginning to take shape, and the girls were visualising themselves in the flowing robes of former centuries. Sheila's mother had written a pleasant letter inviting Christine to her home for the Christmas holidays, and had received a stilted and rather ungracious note of acceptance from that young person. Between rehearsals and hockey practice there was very little time to spare and the days raced by until it was the afternoon for the cycling outing.

An excited group gathered in the Green Court soon after one-thirty, and after Margaret had issued a few necessary instructions they set forth. The Sussex fields were looking their loveliest in the Autumn sunlight, and Sheila felt her heart lift. The past year had been an anxious one, while her sister's health had been so precarious, and this was the first time that Sheila realised there was no more need for anxiety; she could enjoy the quiet countryside in peace. She glanced at Christine, pedalling away beside her on a brand new model bicycle, which showed up her own in all its shabbiness.

How grand to feel that her rebellious little friend was settling down into school routine at last.

"Let's sing while there's no one about," suggested Margaret, and lightheartedly they burst into song, soon forgetting shyness, and waving back at country folk who enjoyed their passing.

As they ascended the hill leading to Maidens Copse their vocal efforts died down; they needed all their breath for the rather gruelling climb. But the view at the top was worth all their trouble. The girls ran about, exclaiming in delight as they regarded the calm beauty of the land which lay beneath them.

"Isn't it glorious!" Margaret said happily. "Just rest or wander about while we arrange about tea. And," she added as an afterthought, "of course you won't go out of sight."

She and Hilda made their way over to the farm-house in the next field and the girls dispersed in groups to enjoy themselves in their own way. The Fourth, always a "cliquey" form walked together until they came to a grassy bowl, and here they flung themselves on the soft turf and rested for a time. Most of them were too active to remain in one place long however, and they wandered away gradually until only Sheila and Christine were left.

"It's a long time since I've seen anything like this," Christine said, waving her hand.

Sheila smiled. "It's not much more than a year since I was here, but I used to think of it sometimes during the worrying time we've been having."

"Was it very bad?" Christine sounded unusually sympathetic.

"Oh, yes. Julie had just got over a serious illness—pleurisy and pneumonia—when she had a shock. Her nurse was knocked down and killed before her eyes. Poor old Julie developed all sorts of things—lung trouble, nerves, oh, it was awful! And she couldn't bear me to go out of her sight in case I got run over too. So mother took us both down to the Isle of Wight. We have a small house there, and although it is let the tenants allowed us to live in some of the rooms. Julie gradually got better—there was no traffic on our part of the beach and she began to lose her dreadful fear. Now, thank goodness, she's quite well again."

"You seem to make a habit of helping lame ducks," Christine shied a pebble down the grassy hill as she spoke.

"Lame ducks!" Sheila echoed indignantly. "My own sister—oh, I see," as Christine's meaning dawned on her. "You're not a lame duck!"

"Yes, I am," Christine answered bitterly, though speech seemed to come to her more easily in this open space. "Everything's wrong about me." She hesitated and then said:

"Does your mother know about me? About my father, I mean?"

Sheila spoke very gently. "Yes, she does, and she just feels very sorry for you, so don't feel awkward about it, will you? Nobody will bother you with questions."

She was rewarded with a soft look of gratitude from the other girl. "It's—it's kind," she murmured huskily. "I haven't seen father since he went away and I haven't heard from him either. He forbade me to write or to try to see him, although he sends me messages sometimes." Two big tears rolled suddenly down her cheeks.

"Don't Christine dear," whispered Sheila. "It will be all right, I know."

"Oh, no. I often wonder how he will feel when he comes out. Mother not here, and no one trusting him—"

"He'll have you. You'll see, he will soon make everything right again," Sheila told her comfortingly. Christine smiled gratefully and dried her eyes, and they sat looking down at the quiet landscape until a bell was heard, summoning them to tea. The girls trouped down to the farmhouse, prepared to do justice to the meal provided for them. But here a check arose.

"One girl missing," announced Hilda in her fussy voice. "How careless, when everybody was warned!"

She set off at a great pace across the field again

—Margaret gazing after her in rather worried fashion—and the girls waited, hungry and impatient. Presently she reappeared, accompanied by Priscilla. The Fourth girls felt rather guilty, for they ought to have looked after their formmate better. Hilda was scolding audibly all the way across the field, and it was evident that Priscilla was becoming exasperated.

"Here she is—Priscilla Westerham," Hilda called out to Margaret and the other Sixth Formers. "A new girl causing all this disturbance. It's disgraceful!"

Margaret sighed. "All right, Hilda," she said. "It *was* thoughtless of you, Priscilla."

"So I've been told, several times," burst out Priscilla, exasperated beyond control. "I should—"

Margaret just looked at her quietly.

"I'm sorry, Margaret," Priscilla apologised.

"Right!" The head girl said briskly. "Now girls, tea." And very willingly did the girls direct their attention to the serious business of eating. Priscilla, turning still hot and angry, found herself looking into a friendly pair of laughing eyes—Christine's.

"Come and sit here," that damsel said, pulling her down into the seat next hers. "Don't take any notice of that chattering magpie."

Priscilla giggled and felt better at once, though she was amazed at Christine's approach. Hunger was stronger than curiosity however, and she was soon, like her companions, tucking into the good things which the farm had managed to provide.

"Now, a quick walk round for a last look at the beauty spots, and then we'll have to go," Margaret announced, when they had finished their meal."

"And mind where you go this time Priscilla," Hilda added severely. "I don't want to have to strain my ankle a second time, looking for you."

Priscilla dug her teeth angrily into her lower lip, but seeing Christine's sardonic grin again in evidence she relaxed and went away with the rest of her form.

"How does it feel?" Christine asked out of the side of her mouth. "You're poaching on my preserves."

"You can have 'em back," the other girl said fervently, "I'm not enjoying them."

And they laughed because they had a common grievance.

Then it was time for the party once again to mount bicycles for the homeward journey, and waving good-bye to the farmer and his wife the girls set off. On, on down still leafy lanes they rode, the dying sun casting a soft glow over the fields. Priscilla, Christine and Sheila rode together, and from that evening the three of them walked together in friendship.

CHAPTER SIX

THE PAGEANT OF GREYCOURT

"Oh dear, I'm so nervous!" wailed Hilda.

"You're nervous? Why you're not even in the show. What about me?" Margaret was fastening a long white veil on her hair as she spoke.

All day long, excitement had reigned at Greycourt. Of course, a holiday had been declared to mark the Centenary, and during the afternoon the school had been thrown open to all local residents, for it was felt that they, as well as their ancestors, had a share in Greycourt history. But it was after the outside public had gone, and only parents and friends remained, that the serious business of entertainment began. And now the School Hall was filled with a pleasantly expectant audience. The stage had been enlarged for the pageant so that the speaking chorus would be able to stand clear of all scenery. "Legend of Greycourt," was to be a pretty lengthy affair, but neither the audience nor the actors minded that, for Greycourt belonged to them and they to Greycourt.

And now the footlights glowed with a soft brilliance. The hall was darkened, and a hush of expectancy was over all as Priscilla, dressed simply in white, took her place at the piano and began at once to play. Priscilla was so used to playing to audiences, that she was not in the least nervous, and enjoyed her music. It was evident that the audience did too, and the Fourth, of course, were tremendously proud of her. As she was nearing the end of her pianoforte solo Priscilla altered the key slightly, and before the audience had grasped what was happening the school song was being sung very softly. Then the singers became discernible through a transparent curtain and, as the song swelled to its ending, the curtain went up, and there on the stage were twenty white-robed maidens singing and putting their hearts into it. Up rose the audience to its feet and joined in, while overhead the noble tones of an organ rolled out the final magnificent chords. The enthusiasm continued while the brilliant lighting changed to a golden hue which illumined the faces of the Chorus, and with the soft throb of the organ for accompaniment they began to speak the first part of the Greycourt story. Then the transparent curtain was before them, the light dimmed— they were gone, and the pageant of Greycourt had begun.

"Isn't it going well!" exclaimed Ronnee softly.

The speaking chorus were in their school uniforms once more, and now, with a large screen to hide them, had taken their places on the steps at the back of the stage.

"Yes, it's lovely. Let's be very quiet," whispered Maureen back, and the girls stood motionless. Miss Dyson appeared when necessary to give them their cue and beat time for them; then she would smile and leave them. There was one flaw in this otherwise perfect evening and that was Hilda. Her ankle had been a little troublesome since the cycling outing, and it was thought that she should not have to put any extra strain on it. So she had rested as much as possible during the past few days and now was walking about with a stick, which she really did not need. This evening she would keep wandering in and out, unable in her nervousness to settle anywhere. When she came round the back of the stage she frowned warningly at the singers and placed her finger on her lips, though none of the girls had any intention of speaking to her. She felt the screen to make sure that it was quite firm and not likely to fall down. She inspected the singers, whereupon Christine promptly made a face at her, which drew forth a shocked "Tut!" But the pageant proceeded on its stately way in spite of her, and Sheila, who was revelling in her part of a medieval maiden, had time for a thrill of pride and satisfaction when she thought of Christine actually taking part in this great song of praise. Surely now she would become a normal schoolgirl! It would be all plain sailing from now, Sheila felt sure.

Meanwhile Hilda was making another of her visitations backstage. The girls looked at one another with resignation but forbore to make any remark. And then Hilda swooped down on Ronnee as she whispered again to Maureen.

"Sh!" she hissed. "Not a word—*please* Veronica."

This was too much for Christine. "Why don't *you* keep quiet?" she said in a hoarse whisper. "You're making more din than the lot of us."

"Well really!" Hilda walked fussily away, obviously upset, but the girls did not dare say anything to Christine. They hoped that Hilda would have the sense to stay away from them for the rest of the "show." And in the meantime there was more singing for them—lovely singing, which was leading up to the final Angelic chorus. Christine was enjoying herself now. All that was best in her came to the front, and she was visualising the scene to which this Angels' Chorus was the accompaniment. Sheila would be standing in a ray of light looking up to Margaret who, halfway up a white stairway would be holding out her arms encouragingly. It was all going so marvellously, thought Christine happily, it was all working so absolutely according to... She "came to" suddenly, as Hilda materialised before her. The senior girl was shaking her head in disapproval of her joyous demeanour. Christine swung from one extreme to another, and in a great rage she lunged forward and gave Hilda a vigorous push. There was a sudden catch in the girls' voices as Hilda staggered backwards, tripping over her stick as she did so, and then, with a crash, the screen toppled over!

Miss Meredith, who had been enjoying the beauty of the Pageant, and the angels' songs, which had seemed to be coming nearer every moment, gripped her programme tightly as the draped screen toppled over, revealing very ordinary "angels" standing on wooden steps, and looking by no means angelic. She bowed her head as a ripple of laughter ran round the hall, and though she was glad to hear that the girls were carrying on as if nothing had happened, the pleasure of the evening was spoiled for her.

At the end of the performance, the audience clapped and cheered as if to make up for its lapse into hilarity, and Miss Meredith, going on to the stage, acknowledged their applause in her gracious way. She spoke of Greycourt past and present, and praised the production just completed.

"Although our 'angels' made rather an unorthodox appearance," she remarked, amid much laughter, "I am hoping that the general performance will have obliterated that particular part of it. It certainly gave a note of novelty to the proceedings!" And, once again acknowledging the applause, the headmistress descended from the stage. The evening was virtually over then and the guests were soon dispersing.

Miss Meredith vanished to her own domain, the hall lights were put out; the girls went in to supper. On the surface it seemed as if everything had returned to normal, but it was on the surface only. Although they said nothing to her, the Fourth were seething with indignation towards Christine, and for the first time that young lady felt something like panic, for she knew she had spoiled the play. She almost wished the girls would abuse her; it would be easier to bear than this complete silence. Even Sheila would not meet her eyes. She supposed Sheila was finished with her at last. Oh, well, hadn't she warned her about being friendly? Only— only, school hadn't seemed quite as bad lately and she hadn't meant to lose her temper.

The same unearthly silence continued for the rest of the evening, and Christine was glad to go to bed. Then Priscilla, who had seen the accident from the front and thought it very funny—Priscilla passed her in the dormitory and called out "'Night Christine!" and Christine's hot rebellious little heart was eased somewhat. Not everyone condemned her, and she crept into bed feeling less lonely than she had expected.

CHAPTER SEVEN

AFTERMATH

Two girls were having a bad quarter of an hour in Miss Meredith's room; they were Hilda and Christine. The Headmistress had not much time to spare, but the amount of subject matter which she packed into the few minutes gave the girls furiously to think for some time to come.

Christine was dealt with first. She hated having to go to Miss Meredith, because she was made to feel that it was mean and contemptible of her to take advantage of her position. Without actually saying so, Miss Meredith conveyed to her the fact that she had been received and treated in the most kindly manner at Greycourt—a school which could choose its pupils from many aspirants, and that she had repaid this kindness with base ingratitude. When the girls said something like this to her, Christine only laughed and retorted rudely, but Miss Meredith had such a quiet, effective way of putting things that she pierced even Christine's self-sufficiency, and it

was as much as the girl could do to stand rigidly
and not show that she cared at all; for she would
have died rather than show any emotion. Indeed,
it was Hilda, who had not been addressed at all
yet, who was weeping copiously. She had never
seen the headmistress in this light before. Miss
Meredith was usually so understanding, even
when she had to administer a rebuke. Hilda
waited in something like terror for her turn.
But after the door had closed upon a white-
lipped Christine, Miss Meredith turned towards
Hilda, and her brow relaxed.

"Sit down, dear," she said quietly. "Don't
cry any more. I am sure that you had no intention
of causing such a disturbance last night."

Hilda looked up, surprised, the tears still wet
on her cheeks. "I?" she stammered. "Why,
Miss Meredith, I didn't. I was pushed—"

Miss Meredith shook her head. "I'm afraid
you must take some blame, Hilda. Christine
should have controlled her temper. I am not
excusing her. But if you had not interfered
unnecessarily she would not have been tempted."

Hilda looked slightly offended. "I'm—I'm
sorry, Miss Meredith," she said, with a suspicion
of a sniff. "I was only doing my duty. I thought
we in the Sixth were supposed to help when we
could."

The headmistress looked kindly at her. "You
are right dear, and I am always glad when my

girls use their initiative and act in the interest of the school. But you must use common sense as well. Have the right approach. Don't antagonise the younger girls. You will find that most of them will respond to a reasonable appeal, but they will resent it at once if you speak in a dictatorial manner." The headmistress hesitated for a moment, then added, "Will you try especially to be patient with Christine? She needs a great deal of help, I assure you, from her school-fellows. You can help her more than I."

Hilda nodded gratefully at this mark of confidence. "Yes, I promise I will, Miss Meredith. I'll try not to worry her again."

And Miss Meredith smiled, well pleased as she hurried off to her lecture.

Meanwhile Sheila had had time to become thoroughly ashamed of herself for deserting her friend, and when Christine came into the form room, looking white and furious, she felt more guilty than ever. Only get this lesson over and she'd talk to Christine somehow, even if she had to break a rule to do it! But the fates were against her. Mademoiselle, who usually took several minutes to get across to the Fourth, to-day arrived just as their form mistress was leaving. At midday, Sheila waited outside the form room but was dismayed to see Mlle Henri and Christine come out together and walk away in the opposite direction.

Miss Meredith, who seldom gave a punishment, had told Christine that she would have to pay a penalty for having let the school down on such an important occasion; so Christine was not to speak to her school-fellows or be in their company for the rest of the day. Actually, she sat in a comfortable little room, with a fire burning brightly, and plenty of books, and she pretended to herself that she liked this better than ordinary school. The afternoon outside was cold, and a dismal wind was howling around the corners. Christine grinned wickedly as she chose a book and settled herself comfortably by the fire. She read contentedly until the light began to fail, and then sat lazily gazing into the fire. This was nice. It reminded her of the winter afternoons when Mother would be upstairs resting before tea and she would be sitting in the firelight waiting for Father. He'd put his head around the door and say, "Doesn't *anyone* love me?" and she'd aim a cushion at him and— oh! oh! *Oh!* Christine clapped her hand over her mouth to prevent herself from crying out loud. She blinked her eyelids rapidly. She must *not* cry. She must not think! So she jumped up quickly, switched on the light and opened her book determinedly and later, when tea was brought, she preserved an indifferent attitude. But the evening seemed to go twice as slowly and she no longer wanted to read.

Supper was brought to her by Flo, her friend of the kitchen. The maid set out the meal and then remained for a gossip.

"You've had a long day of it, haven't you," she remarked sympathetically. "Never mind. Soon be over now."

Somehow it wasn't half the fun having kitchen folk to visit her, as it was when she visited them. She murmured an answer to Flo, and went on eating her supper.

Flo leaned back familiarly and continued, "Wasn't it a lark last night? We were up in the gallery and saw it all. Matter of fact, we were gettin' a bit tired of it. Give me the Pictures any day; it was a bit too highbrow for my taste. But when that screen fell over, and there you all were in your everyday frocks, well, Cook and me just crept out and had a good laugh. Some of 'em think they're so wonderful—it just served them right to—"

Christine sat up stiffly. "It doesn't seem funny to me," she said curtly. "I'd rather not talk about it now."

Flo bridled indignantly. "Oh, very well, I know when I'm not wanted," she declared and she flounced out of the room in high dudgeon. In the kitchen she told her particular friend that Christine "had put on airs ever since she took up with that Sheila."

Christine shrugged her shoulders. Now she

had offended Flo, and upon reflection it did seem silly to have flared up when the maid was running down the school. She, Christine, had often done it herself. "There's one thing," she thought, "I'll never grumble about prep. again. It does make the evening go." And she was heartily glad when the time came for her release. She scampered upstairs, and was in bed and asleep before the others came up.

The next morning, Sheila made her way over shyly but determinedly.

"Oh, I'm glad you're here again," she said.

"Really?" Christine spoke in a light, detached tone. "So I'm back in favour, am I?"

"Please don't, Christine. I was ever so sorry you got into trouble, but I must admit I was cross with you for spoiling the show. It's over now; let's forget it."

Christine shrugged. "Suits me. Perhaps you'll stop trying to reform me now."

Before Sheila could reply, the bell rang for morning school. But Sheila had no intention of relinquishing her purpose, and now that the initial awkwardness of "making it up" with Christine was over she vowed that she would not again lose patience with her friend. Consequently, Christine was propelled, protesting, to the hockey field that afternoon. Indeed, Christine was not the only one who protested.

"Sheila, this is going a bit too far," grumbled

Janet. "I do think we ought to show her what we think of her for letting everyone down like that." And the rest of the girls were inclined to agree.

"She's been shown," retorted Sheila warmly, "She had all day yesterday to think about it, as well as an interview with Merry. Do give her a chance."

"Trouble with you is you never know when you're beaten," Ronnee told her with an exhausted sigh. "All right girls, let's play ball again with our sweet little Christine."

Laughing, the girls got into their appointed places. Although they had not had many practices they were getting into good shape again, and Miss Duncan, the coach, gave them an approving nod as she passed them on her way to the Fifth.

Presently, Hilda came along, but instead of noticing the improvement in their play she noticed a number of blazers and woolly coats flung down carelessly on the grass. She held up her hand for practice to stop.

"Really you girls," she bleated, "it's too bad of you to leave your coats about like this. Do try to remember you are in the senior school now. Come at once."

The Fourth formers obeyed without answering, though they deeply resented the "At once." Christine watched them scornfully, but made no attempt to pick up her own blazer. Hilda looked at her uncertainly for a moment, then walked away without taking any further action.

"At least she didn't get her own way there," muttered Ronnee with satisfaction, and the Fourth looked more kindly on their "pest" in consequence.

"You're doing very well," Sheila told Christine as they came off the field together. "When we go home we'll try to get some practice in with the local team. They're good. Eh? What's the matter now?"

Christine was frowning in a puzzled way. "Oh, you won't want me to come home with you. Not after the other night. It's all right. I understand."

"Don't you want to come?"

"That isn't the point. What I'm saying is—"

"A lot of rot," finished Sheila emphatically if not elegantly. "You're invited home for Christmas and don't you try to wriggle out of it."

Christine laughed. "Oh, all right, all right! I'll save my breath, you just won't listen. I'll come, but don't say I didn't warn you."

"I'm not scared," Sheila said comfortably. "We'll risk it."

CHAPTER EIGHT

TOO CLEVER

Everything seemed to fall flat in the days that followed the pageant, and it was fortunate that the Christmas holidays were drawing near. School was comparatively peaceful because everybody was occupied with the business of learning or teaching, and there was a great deal of work to be got through before the end of term. The large hall was commandeered for the usual examinations, and the school held its social gatherings in the study hall. It was there that Priscilla began to improvise verses to go with her music, and, as she never minded doing it all over again in their Common Room, the Fourth graciously allowed her to amuse the rest of the school. But since the cycling outing, Priscilla preferred to be with Sheila and Christine, with whom she had struck up such a friendship. She liked them, both, but she found Christine irresistible and was more than willing to support her in any mischief that might be afoot. However, Sheila, by keeping a weather eye on Christine, was able also to steer Priscilla along the straight and narrow path.

Then, one cold afternoon, when Sheila had to go to music practice, the other two decided to skip the afternoon walk; that is, Christine suggested doing so and Priscilla agreed enthusiastically. As a general rule it wasn't difficult to do this, for the mistress who accompanied them usually left them pretty much alone once she had checked them out. This afternoon, Miss Masterson, their form mistress, was in charge, and she didn't even check their names to begin with. So, as soon as they deemed it safe, the two scuttled away and hid until the rest of the girls were out of sight. Then they emerged cautiously.

"Where now?" Priscilla asked, her eyes bright with mischief.

"I've never been in the village on a weekday," Christine said. "We walk through it on Sunday going to Church, but it's dead as a doornail then. Let's go and look at the fancy shop. It always looks intriguing when we pass it."

So, to the fancy shop they went, by the simple expedient of climbing over a low gate leading from the ancient part of Greycourt into the lane which ran down to the churchyard. They feasted their eyes on the pretty goods displayed in the shop window, which was decked in gay attire for the approaching festive season. Priscilla tired of this after a time.

"Is this the main street of the village?" she wanted to know. "Can't we walk along a bit?"

"This is *all* the village; there aren't any other streets, and since all the houses you can see are occupied by mistresses and overflow courtiers I don't think we'll venture that way, my child!"

Priscilla's eyes were very round. "Whew! I should say not!" she exclaimed. "Let's get back."

"Yes, it's frightfully cold. Let's wait for a minute—see if there's anyone about. Do you know this road is supposed to be haunted?"

"No! Tell me."

"Oh, the story is that of a horseman who came galloping down this very road to announce the news that some battle had been lost. I think he just lived long enough to warn the villagers. They say that whenever bad news is coming to Greatoaks, you hear the clip-clop of horses' hooves down the village street."

"Ugh!" shivered Priscilla. "How scarifying! Let's get back, eh?"

"Yes, I think it's safe now."

The two girls scampered back to the warm school building, and soon were chuckling over their cleverness in dodging the cold walk. They were not to go scot free however. Miss Masterson, reaping the benefit of past experience, had purposely left the checking of the girls' names until their return, and it was not long before she was confronting the culprits.

"Have you any excuse to offer for evading the walk?" she asked them.

They hadn't, of course.

"Very well." The mistress made a note on her list and left them without another word.

"What—what's she going to do?" gasped Priscilla.

"Report to Miss Meredith, mean old thing. It's considered a serious offence here to dodge walks." Christine glanced sideways at her companion. "See what you get for associating with me!"

"I wouldn't have missed it!" Priscilla declared stoutly. "I enjoyed every minute. What'll happen?"

"Pi-jaw from Merry for you. Same without any frills for me. I'm considered a hopeless case. And I expect we'll be done out of the Christmas party."

"Oh!" Priscilla's mouth went down at the corners, but she recovered immediately. "Never mind—plenty at home. I expect Sheila will go for us don't you?"

An unexpected dimple appeared near Christine's firm lips. "No, Sheila will be patient and understanding. She won't say a word of blame."

And Sheila didn't. When she heard about their escapade she just looked sympathetic, and then began to talk of something else; at which her two graceless friends exchanged a chuckle.

But Miss Masterson was not quite the mean old thing that Christine thought her. True, the lapse with regard to this particular rule had to be reported, but the mistress had her own way of managing these affairs.

"I have several reports to send in to you, Miss Meredith," she said gravely, but with twinkling eyes, "but I would prefer to send them in to you next Monday if that meets with your approval."

"That will do beautifully." Miss Meredith spoke gravely too, but strange to relate, her eyes seemed to sparkle also. "We'll get the party over first, shall we?"

CHAPTER NINE

CHRISTMAS AT WHITE GATES

"There, that's White Gates—through the trees —see?" Sheila parted some branches. "Jolly old home—MUM!"

"You madcap!" exclaimed her mother, hurrying down the steps to kiss her daughter. "Do you want to disturb the whole neighbourhood?"

"Oh, Mums, it *is* good to be home again. When I get to the last few days before breaking up, I don't know how to stand it. This is Christine, Mum dear. Christine, my mother," she announced with a proud flourish.

Mrs. Conway greeted Christine cordially. Her children had always brought their friends home and Mrs. Conway was well versed in the art of entertaining young folks. "You're just in time for tea," she said. "Slip upstairs with Sheila, my dear, she'll show you your room. I'll wait for you."

Christine's room was a pretty little one, next to Sheila's and she glanced about, pleased with what she saw. Now that the ordeal of meeting

Sheila's mother was over, she felt she was going to enjoy herself. And then she caught sight of the letter propped up on the mantelshelf and she frowned as she recognised Mrs. Cameron's writing.

"Dear Christine," the letter ran,
"I was so glad when Miss Meredith let me know about your invitation. I am only too happy that you will have a beautiful Christmas. I know that your birthday comes at this time, and am adding a little to my Christmas gift; please do get something you like. You already know that I should like you to come to us for all your holidays, but until the idea appeals to you, I shall not ask you to do this. If you change your mind, do come; we could have some good fun together.

This is what you'll want to know. Your father sends you his love. He is not unhappy and is being treated considerately. He is determined to begin again and looks forward to getting his affairs settled. He adds that you, like himself, are quick-tempered, and that he knows how trying all this must be for you. Hold on, and he will try to make it all up to you later on.

Your father is very brave isn't he? For he is having to fight against some injustice, though he is the first to admit that he was partly to blame. You be brave too, and before you know where you are, your troubles will be behind you.

Every good and happy wish for Christmas. Little Joan sends you a kiss.

Yours sincerely,

DOLORES CAMERON."

A generous sum of money was enclosed. Christine, with her lips firmly pressed together, slipped the letter into a drawer, and went down to tea with Sheila, but Mrs. Conway, in spite of all her efforts, found it impossible to draw Christine into the general conversation, and the kind lady began to feel quite exhausted.

"Now we want to have a look round, Mummy," Sheila said, with a grateful smile at her mother. "You rest now and don't bother about us any more."

"*I* don't want to be a bother to anyone," Christine roused herself to remark.

Mother and daughter hastened to assure her that she was no bother, that it was a pleasure to have her with them, and that they only wanted her to have a good time, but when the girls had gone from the room, Mrs. Conway sat down again and gazed rather thoughtfully at the fire.

After a quick inspection of pet rabbits and the dogs, the two girls ran up to Julie's room, where the sisters had a somewhat boisterous reunion. Julie was a pretty rather delicate-looking girl, and her blue eyes danced at times with mischief.

She still had to rest each afternoon, though the doctors were pleased with her progress.

"Here she is, Christine; my young sister Julie. We've got three great brothers, but they won't be home till to-morrow."

"Come and sit here," commanded Julie and her visitors sat down obediently while she bombarded them with questions. She was curious about Christine and showed it, but somehow Christine did not mind her inquisitiveness and answered her questions patiently. Julie seemed quite sorry when the girls had to go.

At the evening meal, Christine sat so quietly that Mrs. Conway decided she must be tired and suggested bed. To her relief, the girl agreed at once and after a stilted good night went from the room. Sheila and her mother looked at each other silently for a moment or two, then Sheila spoke.

"Don't judge her just yet, Mummy," she pleaded. "I know she's a bit awkward at times, but she's ever so much better than she was."

Her mother sighed. "I have to think of others as well, Sheila my dear. You can't expect us all to keep on making allowances for her, now can you?"

Sheila shook her head in complete agreement. "Course not, Mummy. I'll keep her out of the way when she's in a difficult mood. Don't you worry."

But Mrs. Conway could be firm too. "Now listen to me, Sheila. If that child doesn't intend to behave herself, she'd better go back to where she comes from. Moods indeed! What next, from a child of fifteen. No, Sheila, no. I'm not having any nonsense, and I'm not going to let you spoil your holiday running round after a person with moods. Understand?"

Sheila was rather tired herself, so she just said, "That's all right, Mummy. Good night," and took herself off to bed.

The next morning at breakfast Christine was charming, and Sheila breathed a sigh of pleasure. Christine in a pretty dress, and with a smile lighting up her intelligent face, was a very different person from the scowling girl of last night. But Mrs. Conway remained firm in a kindly way, and Christine found it advisable to conform to the customs of the household.

There was uproar when the boys came home. Christine, suddenly shy, ran into a little room off the hall, but one of the boys caught sight of her, and rushed in unceremoniously.

"What are you hiding for?" he demanded. "Hallo, Christina!"

"Christine," she corrected, giving him her hand rather shyly.

"Okay," he grinned. "Hoy, you chaps, this is Christine, Sheila's pal."

"All hail, Queen Christiana of Denmark!"

was Owen's greeting, and "'Lo, Chris," shrilled Denis, the youngest.

"H-hallo," returned Christine, hoping every moment that Sheila would appear, but for once Sheila was missing.

"Just time to see the thingummies," announced John. "Coming, Chris?"

Christine gave up any attempt to assert herself in the face of superior odds and accompanied the boys meekly to see the thingummies, which proved to be the dogs and rabbits. To her surprise she enjoyed herself very much, and she had recovered sufficiently by the end of the afternoon to give them as good as she got in the way of badinage.

"Coo! You've got a lot of go in you for a girl!" exclaimed Owen. "I bet you keep 'em alive at school."

Christine laughed and ran off to join Sheila, but life took on a new zest from that day, and she wasn't given time to indulge in moods, even if she had wanted to do so.

Christmas Day dawned bright and cold, and the whole family, including the noisy brothers, set off for Church. Then followed the traditional Christmas dinner. Whoops from the boys as the turkey appeared, cheers from them all for the Christmas pudding, and a solemn moment when they all stood and drank a toast to their gallant father, killed in the war. Then while the

boys went out to walk off the effects of their
enormous meal, the girls remained with Julie
in the cosy lounge, and talked or read as their
fancy led them. So the quiet Christmas Day
rolled on, and after tea the family began to
bestir itself for the evening's festivities. The
girls got quite excited, dressing up, and Christine's eyes were like stars, as she descended the
stairs in her rose-tinted dress.

It was a grand party, with all the Christmas
games and songs and dances. Everybody ate too
much, but seemed to suffer no ill effects. Boys
and girls, boys and girls—there seemed no end
to them, Christine thought in bewildered delight,
and everyone of them so friendly! All too soon
the party came to an end, and the guests were
saying good-byes to the girls who stood at the
foot of the stairs.

"Coming skating to-morrow, Christine?"

"No, come dancing."

"We're having an unexpected party—do come,"
called out one merry-faced girl, "all the crowd
will be there."

"May we, Mother?" Sheila asked.

Mrs. Conway looked around her. "Yes, dear,
if Sally's mother agrees."

"Moth-er," shrieked Sally to her parent who
was at the other end of the hall. "Please invite
the Conways and Christine to-morrow."

Sally's mother looked at Mrs. Conway and

laughed. "If you care to trust them with my mad crowd, they are very welcome."

Mrs. Conway smiled her thanks. "I'd rather have your 'mad' crowd than some of the so-called demure ones. What time?" And while the mothers discussed pros and cons, their children executed a solemn, if ridiculous, *pas de quartre* on the door step.

"It's the first real party I've been to since my —since—" Christine paused, but her friend cut in quickly with:

"Well, I'm glad you've enjoyed it."

"It's been lovely; every minute of it."

"I'm so glad, I've loved it too. O-ooh, I'm tired!"

They straggled contentedly up to bed and slept soundly until an advanced hour in the morning, when there was the luxury of breakfast in bed. A brisk walk before lunch was followed by a quiet afternoon, and then once again there was the exciting business of dressing up for the party.

"I wish the girls at school could see her now," thought Sheila proudly, as later she watched Christine dancing. The evening was flying by, but it was all very jolly, and the youthful hosts and hostesses went out of their way to give the visitors a good time. Christine was by now the centre of an admiring crowd; she was telling them about the screen falling down at the pageant, and they were all hooting with laughter. Sheila laughed herself, and then slipped into another room to have a few words with an Isle of Wight crony. They sat talking happily until it was time to go in to supper.

"Coo!" exclaimed the boys, as the young people sat down to a Christmassy meal, and it was generally agreed that Sally's mother had "done them proud." For the first few moments everybody was occupied with the serious business of eating, but as the first pangs of hunger wore off, tongues began to wag again."

"A little bit of orlrite, as they say in Bonstead," declared George Rae, replete with food and satisfaction. Then came the shock.

"What do you mean, Bonstead?" demanded Christine, red in face, her eyes furious.

"Wot do I mean, lidy?" George put on a hoarse voice. He thought Christine was acting like himself. "Wot I means is this 'ere. It's as nice a bit er tripe and onions as I've tasted this twelve-month, and if yer arsks me—"

"Oh, shut up," Christine said coldly. "You make me ill."

There was a burst of laughter, if of rather shocked laughter, for the party still thought that George and Christine were acting. Only Sheila was on edge. She was familiar with the expression on Christine's face, and it boded no good.

"Let's dance, shall we?" she said hurriedly.

A chorus of protest arose. "No! We haven't finished yet."

"Stop it, young Sheila," this from her partner. So she gave it up and hoped for the best. At the other end of the table the going was fast and furious. George was pretending to be a cockney, and Christine was really being rude. The uproar grew to such proportions, that Sally's mother popped her head around the door, but seeing that the guests were laughing, she withdrew.

At last the meal was over and Sheila rose from the table thankfully; she would go over to Christine and stay with her for the rest of the evening. Her mother would be angry if there were any disturbance.

Over she went, as quickly as she could, but alas, not quickly enough. As she reached the group, Christine lifted her hand and struck George across the face!

A more surprised boy than George can scarcely be imagined. He simply could not grasp what was the matter, and to add to the confusion, Sally's mother appeared again at this identical moment. She was horrified.

"Whatever—what on earth—" she began.

George laughed in an embarrassed fashion. "Oh, sorry, Mrs. Dorlan. We were just fooling about. Sorry it got rough house."

Mrs. Dorlan's face cleared. "Oh, I see."

But Christine broke in: "No, we weren't

fooling. He's just a snob, and I'll hit him again if he makes fun of Bonstead. What right has he?"

Poor George! He was completely out of his depth. "Bonstead? What's she mean. Don't know it. I didn't say a word—"

"You did—you did! You've been sneering at them all the time. Well, I come from there, see? And I know which I'd rather have, them or you—you stupid—"

Mrs. Dorlan and Sheila stepped forward.

"I'm terribly sorry," murmured Sheila to her hostess. "Come along, Christine, it's time we were going."

Christine flung up her head, and walked out of the room without another word, and Sheila, after a few apologetic words to the party in general, followed her to the dressing-room. There they put on their wraps in silence and then walked the short distance home. Already Christine's anger had cooled, and she was realising that she had spoiled the party, to say nothing of letting her friend down. She wished irritably that Sheila would fly at her instead of being so forbearing. But Sheila was feeling almost sick with disappointment and could not have flown at anyone.

To their relief, however, Mrs. Conway was not angry. She made the girls have a hot drink and advised them to go to sleep and forget all about the affair.

Christine had a sudden wild desire to apologise for the trouble she had caused, but no words would come, and she followed Sheila without speaking. Nevertheless when, next morning, her hostess proposed that she should write a little note of apology to Mrs. Dorlan, Christine fell in at once with the suggestion and sent off a nicely worded letter that same morning. And that seemed to ease the situation. In a day or two the whole affair had blown over. They went to the Pantomime, and to one or two Christmas shows, but when invitations came for parties, Christine always asked to be excused, and Mrs. Conway supported her, despite all Sheila's pleadings. Julie had become very fond of Christine and the girls spent many afternoons and evenings together when Sheila was invited out.

Strangely enough, it was the boys who made Christine feel that her behaviour had put her beyond the pale. They just weren't going to risk another scene, and so they gave her a wide berth. She felt this keenly, and missed their companionship, and she was glad enough to return to Greycourt when the time came. Mrs. Conway saw the two girls off, but though she remained cordial and imperturbable and though she was grateful to Christine for giving so much time to Julie, Christine guessed that she was relieved that the end of the holiday had come.

CHAPTER TEN

PRISCILLA PLAYS HOCKEY

"And now-hockey," said Sheila firmly.

"Oh *no*-not again!"

"Yes, again. We're not going to let the Lower walk over us if I can help it."

There was one loud concerted groan, and then the Fourth turned out to practise for the coming match with the Lower Fourth. It was no use grumbling. They knew Sheila would keep talking at them until they made a start.

"Now, take your places please, and try to think this is the real thing. Oh bother, where's Ronnee?"

Priscilla laughed. "She's escaped your clutches this afternoon. She's gone to River Cottage."

Sheila tut-tutted, but did not lose any time.

"Come on, Christine," she called out, "you take Ronnee's place. Let's get on with it."

Christine obediently fell into line with the others and soon the game was in full swing. Indeed a large proportion of the school was out on the field that day, for Greycourt had become conscious-stricken on its poor showing for sports the previous year. The Fourth were playing very well, and Sheila's hopes were rising. She was particularly pleased with Christine. Her friend had taken to hockey as a duck to water, and her runs and passes were really brilliant. Only—Sheila sighed—no one would agree to let her play in any match. They'd do a great deal for Sheila, but drew the line there. They couldn't trust Christine not to let them down, and they simply were not taking the risk. So Priscilla was being given special coaching as a reserve, but she was not shaping very well up till now. She remarked on it later to Christine as they sat together at tea.

"I'm a dud at hockey, aren't I? Why on earth are they making me reserve?"

"Cos there's no one else," Christine told her in matter-of-fact tones.

"Oh yes there is. There's you. You can make circles round me. Why—"

"Me? Oh," Christine laughed lightly. "I spoil things, didn't you know? I'd be sure to let the side down if they played me."

"What rot!" Priscilla cried loyally. "The screen was an accident, and we were all in the flypaper, and the open window was just thought-lessness—yes, it was," for Christine was grinning wickedly. "You *ought* to be the reserve. I'm going to propose it."

C.O.F.   F

Christine tossed her unruly curls. "Oh, no you won't. I wouldn't play for them anyway." Then seeing Priscilla's face lengthen, she added, "But I'll help you to practise that stick-swing if you like. You're not bad otherwise."

"Oh, will you really? After tea?" cried Priscilla, who was anxious to acquit herself well if she were needed.

"Yes, after tea and whenever you like," promised Christine and she kept her word. Many times during the following week the girls worked hard practising, and Priscilla began to swing her stick with confidence. Sheila did not see a great deal of her friend these days. Christine had seemed to avoid her since they had come back to school, but she was glad that Christine was keeping out of trouble. True, there had been one or two troublesome incidents already, but they had been of a kind that amused the girls, instead of infuriating them. Christine really seemed to be making an effort at last, and Sheila was content to remain in the background until she was needed.

CHAPTER ELEVEN

LIGHT AND SHADE

The Fourth were spending a quiet afternoon in their common room, as the weather made it impossible to go out of doors. Connie was deep in *Jane Eyre*, Sheila was knitting gloves for Julie's birthday. Maureen was twiddling the knobs of the wireless, though she kept the volume down. Christine was making a ball out of a skein of silk for Sheila. For once the Fourth really did look happy and peaceful as they sat in the firelit room on the cold wintry day. Not until dusk came on did any of them stir. Then Connie jumped up and put the lights on.

"How's Jane?" asked Ronnee.

Connie wrinkled her forehead. "Well, she's not as convincing later on in the book. The first part is fascinating, but she starts to lay the law down later on about all sorts of things."

"Like all school marms," called Maureen from her corner. Connie smiled and settled down to read again and Priscilla drifted over to the piano. She played softly to herself for a time, but gradually the girls gave up what they had been doing, and listened to her. After a few moments, she grinned and began to sing softly to the tune of "Polly-wolly-doodle."

> "Oh the Fourth Form is a lovely form,
>   Except for you *and* you.
> We're always free from stress and storm,
>   And *we* like Irish Stoo!"

"Ugh! How could you, 'Cilla," groaned Connie.

"Can you do better?" inquired that young lady.

"I don't know. Let's see—er—

> "It's a decent form, I do agree,
>   But Irish Stew—what fudge!
> As to who's nice, my good new girl,
>   It's not for you to judge!"

"Hoighty-toighty!" grinned Priscilla, but the rest of the girls loudly applauded Connie's effort.

"Go on," they urged, and nothing loth, Priscilla improvised for several more verses. What they would have felt like, if they had known their form mistress was listening to them, it is difficult to imagine, but as Miss Masterson came hurrying along the corridor, she heard her own name.

"Now Miss Masterson, she's not too bad,
  Though she doesn't often see a joke.
But what can you expect when she likes long
  walks,
It's really time that up she woke!"

Priscilla was singing, and under cover of the squeal of laughter which followed, Miss Masterson tiptoed away, smiling broadly—certainly an inopportune moment to deliver a message, she thought. Anyway, as the tea bell summoned the laughing girls, they little knew that they had had an audience.

The next morning, after school, Miss Masterson gave Christine the deferred message, and a few minutes later Sheila found her in a great rage.

"I absolutely despise her! Horrible, hateful interfering creature!"

"Christine, don't!" exclaimed Sheila. "You know you don't mean it."

"I do, I do!" stormed Christine, shaking back her hair angrily. "Why doesn't she leave me alone? Dental treatment indeed! I suppose if I smirked, or toadied to her, she'd let me off. This is her way of getting even with me. Coward — that's what she is."

"Oh, Christine, don't be silly. You know well enough that we all have to have our teeth attended to. Mrs. Cameron merely agreed to it."

"Very good of her!" But Sheila was glad to

see that her friend was looking a little shame-faced. "It's all very well for you, Shee. They're *my teeth*. I wish people would mind their own business."

Sheila sighed. Christine *was* Mrs. Cameron's business but it was of no use to argue about it now or at any other time. Mrs. Cameron, the charming American lady who had been respon-sible for placing Christine at Greycourt, was surely, of all persons, entitled to respect, if not gratitude, from her; but Christine only felt resentment towards her. And now, with regard to her teeth, Christine was no coward, but she had decided to "hate" Mrs. Cameron, and she was able to whip up her anger with this latest excuse.

"Have you finished deliberating on me and my faults?" drawled Christine, and Sheila realised that she had been day-dreaming. She jumped up.

"I want to look at the notice-board," she said, making for the door and holding it open. "Come on."

"No," Christine said bluntly and she turned away. Sheila was usually long-suffering, but this morning she felt she had put up with enough from Christine. Quietly she closed the door behind her and joined the rest of the Fourth, leaving Christine to her own devices. And after a while Christine discovered that it was no fun nursing a grievance in private and she also joined the girls. But in her perverse way she was determined not to give Sheila the satisfaction of thinking she had prevailed and she ran up to Priscilla and suggested a game on their own. Nothing loth, Priscilla went off with her, and they played fast and furiously until Christine forgot her grievance, and, though she still would not walk with Sheila, she pulled her hair-ribbon off and tossed it at her.

"I suppose I'm to take that to mean that I'm forgiven for whatever it is I've done," thought Sheila, smiling ruefully as she tied up her plait again.

But after tea, Christine's black mood returned, and she walked off bad-temperedly by herself. "If I don't want my teeth seen to, why can't they leave them alone," she told herself fiercely. "Whose teeth are they? I'm not a slave!" Then she jumped.

"Stop muttering in your beard," came Maureen's gay voice suddenly at her side. "Here's a letter for you, delivered by my own fair hands."

"Oh—er—thanks," Christine said hurriedly. "I'll go outside and read it."

"Outside? You're crazy. You can't go out now."

"Who says so?" truculently.

Maureen shrugged. "Oh, you're impossible; it's no use," and she went off disgustedly.

"I *will* go out now," Christine said aloud, and

went to the cloakroom for her coat as the weather
was cold. Curiosity prevailed, however, while
she was there, and she opened her letter. It was
from Flo's mother, the kindly woman who
had befriended her after her father had left her.
A cheering, wholesome letter which brought the
writer's motherly face before Christine. "If you
ever want to come up for a change," she read
through stinging tears, "you'll be heartily welcome, my dear. We're rough and ready, but you
know that. I hope you don't grieve too much
now for your dear Ma. It was a happy release
for her and you mustn't wish her back. It's
your Pa I'm sorry for. He must miss you sore.
Mrs. Cameron has been a real friend, and I am
sure she will help him when he comes out."
Christine gritted her teeth. Oh, yes, she too was
sure that Mrs. Cameron would have a finger in
that pie as well! The letter ended with a friendly
good wish and the invitation to "come whenever
you like; we'll be glad to see you.

Your friend,

Mrs. Peters."

Christine stood quite still for a moment.
Then deliberately she turned to her locker,
changed into heavy walking-shoes, slipped her
purse into her pocket, put her school hat on,
then took it off again and hung it on its peg.
She shut her locker and made her way quietly

out of the building. Then, in a panic, she took to her heels and ran—out of the gates of Greycourt, down the one street of the village and on, until she was out of breath. As she slowed down, she began to feel cold and she turned up her coat collar and wrapped her scarf around her head. On she trudged, over the rough road, her feet unaccountably heavy, but her temper still blazing nicely. She had been walking for about half an hour when she came to the railway halt for Greycourt, but she couldn't wait there for a train, of course; they'd know at once she was from Greycourt, even though she had left her hat behind. No, she must keep on until she reached Oakstane, the county town for that district, where most of the long-distance bus services touched; and she must do it quickly. "Once I'm up in London, Mrs. Peters won't send me back," she thought. "She'll scold and say I'm a silly girl but…. And even if she makes me go back, I'll have been away from the horrid place for a while. Oh, I'm tired! I wish I could have brought my bicycle."

On, on, through the fading light and, it must be confessed, with fading enthusiasm, Christine walked wearily. She remembered now that her walking-shoes had become a little loose, but the school walks had not been sufficiently long for her to feel much discomfort from them. Now they rasped up and down on her heels, and she

would have given much to rest, but she dared
not. It was about an hour later that she arrived,
footsore and weary, at Oakstane. A hasty glance
at the time-table showed her that there would
not be a London coach for nearly an hour, and
she sank on to a bench, thankful that she would
not have to face anyone just yet.

At Greycourt, Christine was not missed until
supper, when Sheila looked about worriedly.

"Anyone seen Christine?" she asked.

No one had, though Maureen volunteered the
information that she had seen her some time
previously, when, in her pigheaded way, she had
gone out of doors. "Yes," affirmed Maureen in
response to Sheila's exclamation, "she had to go
out, if you please, to read a letter she'd just had.
I told her she was crazy, and that finished me
off, of course."

The others grinned, though they became
serious immediately, and Connie rose to her feet.
"I'd better tell someone, hadn't I?" she asked.
"It's awful to make a fuss, but she wasn't at
prep., and something might have happened to
her."

Sheila and Priscilla looked on anxiously as
Connie made her way over to the prefects' table.
After her first frown of disapproval, they saw
Margaret jump up and speak to Miss Masterson,
and the two left the dining-hall together. It
was not long before search parties were making

off in all directions, and Miss Meredith was telephoning the railway stations. Nothing had been seen of a Greycourt girl at the halt, and no London train had stopped at the main-line station since six-thirty. There would be one at eight-fifteen, and they would watch. In the meantime, Miss Meredith went off in the school car to search on her own. The headmistress's face was grey with anxiety, for all her girls, without exception, were precious charges to her. Now she racked her brains to know how she had failed this child, who had started so happily at Greycourt in spite of her trouble.

"Don't take on, Miss," urged Sam, who in addition to being a gardener and carpenter, also drove the school car. "She'll turn up. They always do."

And Miss Meredith smiled, a little comforted.

It so happened that Margaret's parents were staying in the village for the week-end in order to be with their daughter for a short time. The head girl was always allowed the privilege of these visits, and in its time the old village inn had offered its hospitality to many parents of Head Girls. Now Margaret slipped across to ask for her father's help and Mr. Rainer rose to the occasion. He chartered the village taxi and set off at once.

The time went slowly by. Miss Meredith returned; the gates were closed; the school, with the exception of the Sixth Form and Sheila and Priscilla, had gone to bed. These two had begged so hard to be allowed to remain up that Margaret had obtained permission for them to do so. And so they waited, for hours it seemed, until suddenly Priscilla, who had very keen hearing, held up her hand. "Listen," she said, sounding rather frightened.

But the others as yet could not distinguish any sound.

"What can you hear, Priscilla?" Margaret spoke gently.

"Oh, surely you can hear! It's a horse—galloping. It's coming nearer—oh! The legend —bad news."

Margaret walked over and put her arm round the girl's shoulder. "Don't let that worry you," she said reassuringly. "If there's a horse on the road, there will be a perfectly natural reason for it." But she ended rather abruptly, for now the clip-clop of horse's hooves were distinctly audible to them all. For a brief moment a wave of something like terror surged over them; then common sense came to their aid.

"Cocoa, I think—yes?" Margaret suggested practically, and they all clutched with relief at such an ordinary everyday way of going on. And when the door bell pealed out a few minutes later, not one of them was startled.

Mr. Rainer appeared, carrying Christine in

his arms. "It's all right," he said quickly to Miss Meredith. She's walked her feet into a dreadful state, that's all. Where shall——"

"In here, for to-night." Miss Meredith opened a door as she spoke and the matron and a maid set about making everything comfortable while Christine was placed on a couch for the time being. Mr. Rainer went off in a great hurry, and had almost reached the outer door, when Margaret flew after him and gave him a hug, the like of which he had not had for years.

"Good night, Daddy dear," she said huskily. "I'll never forget it."

"Steady on, lass," he urged, trying not to sound pleased and went off into the night.

Christine had to remain in bed several days until her feet had healed again, but apart from a slight cold, she felt none the worse for her ordeal. She was conscience-stricken, however, at the trouble she had caused. She thought she would never forget the anxiety that was lined into Miss Meredith's face that night, and very promptly she gave her word that never again would she leave school in such a manner.

"But I can't promise not to be bad-tempered," she added apologetically. "I'm just naturally bad-tempered."

"Most of us are," Miss Meredith said, to her surprise. "All I ask you to do, is to make an effort at overcoming it each time. You won't notice any improvement at first, but each effort will make you stronger against it, and after a time you will find it much easier to deal with."

To Sheila and Priscilla, who came to visit her after she had been removed to the San., she related the rest of her escapade.

"I was sitting on a bench, waiting for the coach, when a taxi drew up and Margaret's father came over to me. I tried to walk away but—well, I fell over. My feet seemed as if they couldn't bear any more pain. He begged me not to make a fuss, and then he called old John from the taxi and they both helped me in. I either fainted, or went to sleep for a little while, because I 'came to' suddenly to hear old John carrying on alarmingly! His old taxi had broken down. I don't know how he managed, but we got to the halt somehow, and transferred ourselves to the horse cab. That's about all, I think."

"Except that the horse gave me, at least, a horrible fright," Priscilla said, with feeling. "You know—the legend."

Christine gave a squeal of laughter. "Oh! Poor old 'Cilla. What a shame!"

Sheila rose. "I don't think we ought to stay any longer," she said, "but I'm so glad you're better. Hurry up and come back. I miss you."

Christine regarded her uncertainly, however, as if she still could not make up her mind as to whether Sheila meant what she said.

CHAPTER TWELVE

SPRING FEVER AND DOLORES

Christine entered the form-room with her shoulders hunched defiantly. She didn't intend to stand any nonsense, even if she *had* tried to run away! To her surprise, however, she found she was regarded rather as a heroine than a wrongdoer. Several girls nodded or smiled at her. Ronnee Parnell automatically offered her pencil sharpener as soon as she had finished with it, and Janet pointed out the place in the lesson, which Christine couldn't find at once as she had been away. Of course Sheila was there with her warm smile, and Priscilla gave her a quick mischievous wink as their eyes met. Christine looked around the form-room as if she were seeing it for the first time. It *was* a pleasant room, and the views from the windows were lovely.

As they were changing their shoes in the cloakroom that afternoon, Maureen made a sudden rush at her. "Now don't fly at me," she said, "but I'd just like to tell you I'm sorry if I upset you last week. I'm a bit too quick with my tongue. I know that."

Christine straightened herself up, looked at Maureen, then gulped, "I—I—'er—" she began, and stopped.

"It's all right," Maureen said soothingly. "Consider it said, if you like."

"But I *don't* like!" Christine exploded. "I'm trying to say something too, but it's hard because I've been such a pig. Yes, I have. I went out because you told me not to." Maureen grinned broadly. "But I tried to get away, because the letter made me homesick. So you needn't blame yourself for anything."

Maureen looked relieved. "I'm glad of that anyway. Coming?" And they went off to the playing field together.

Christine had her dental treatment after a few days. It was not at all severe, and soon over. However, perhaps she had not recovered from the long exposure and fatigue of her self-imposed walk, or she may have caught fresh cold in her gums, but towards the end of morning school she discovered that she had a swelling on the left side of her face. In some dismay she placed her hand over the swelling, and managed to escape notice until the class was dismissed. Then she pretended to be busy looking for something in her desk until the rest of the Fourth were on their way downstairs. She followed them slowly, dreading to enter the dining-hall, for she was very sensitive to ridicule in spite of her indifferent manner. As she stood hesitating, the Vice-Captain, Hilda Cartip, came hurrying along.

"Now, Christine, what are you doing?" she demanded. "You know you should be in the dining-hall. Have you washed your hands?"

Christine moved forward, disdaining to answer, but Hilda, with a sudden exclamation, caught her arm.

"Are you eating a sweet? Eating? Upon my word this is a little too much. Eating on the way to lunch. What do you mean—?"

"Oh, go and eat your hat!" Christine shouted, exasperated beyond all endurance.

"Well, *really*! I think I've been very patient with you, Christine Barry, but there is a limit. I won't report you to Miss Meredith this time, but I certainly shall speak to Margaret. Go in to lunch now."

Christine departed, with one of her old rages boiling up within her, and Hilda continued on her hurrying way. It was too bad that she'd had to notice that Barry child. Margaret got irritable if you reported girls too often, but really when a girl stood, with a great bulge in her cheek waiting to finish what she was eating before going into the dining-hall, you simply had to take some notice.

Christine kept her hand to her face as much as

possible and the girls did not remark on the swelling. After lunch, she slipped along to Miss Masterson, who gave one glance at her and took her at once to the San.

"I've brought your patient back again, Matron. She's not quite up to standard yet."

Miss Wills hurried forward. "Come along, Christine. Doctor hasn't been yet. He'll soon put it right for you."

"It doesn't hurt. I'm quite all right," protested Christine, though she spoke stiffly.

"Course you are! But you might as well have your face its normal size, mightn't you? Sit down there by the fire, there's plenty to read."

So Christine received attention from kindly Doctor Atkinson, who came each day to the school, and she was able to be in class next morning, though she was not allowed to go out of doors. Sheila remained with her during the afternoon, but Priscilla played hockey under orders from Christine, though later she joined her friends and amused them with her nonsense. And in the days that followed, the Fourth was at peace.

This halcyonic state of affairs could not last, of course. The Fourth had got out of the way of peace. And Christine had nothing to do with the epidemic of lawlessness which presently broke out. The improving weather and first promise of Spring seemed to bring out any "skittishness" lying dormant among the members of the Fourth. They began to behave in a way which scandalised Sheila, drew forth remonstrances from Connie and even surprised Christine. Hair-ribbons were tweaked off and solemnly handed to their owners. Many letters arrived at the school at this time, but when the recipients opened them eagerly, they found blank sheets of paper. Objects were dropped over the banisters on unfortunate persons below; and after each exploit, the Fourth crowed lustily. It was the same in class. Visiting mistresses all suffered from the Fourth's attack of Spring Fever. It was on the Friday after Christine's return that Miss Yelland, the English mistress, threw down her pencil and gave an exclamation of despair.

"You really are dreadful this morning, Janet. Didn't you learn any of the poem yesterday?"

Janet assumed the fatuous expression so fashionable in the Fourth at present.

"Yesterday, Miss Yelland?" she repeated vaguely. "Do you mean—"

"I mean yesterday," snapped the mistress.

"Oh, *yesterday*! Oh, yes, of course."

"You are being rude, Janet."

Up popped Ronnee. "Oh, no, Miss Yelland," she said in mild expostulation. "Janet isn't rude."

And from various quarters of the room came sweet echoes, each a second after the other.

"Oh, no! Janet isn't rude, Miss Yelland."

"Oh, she *isn't* rude, Miss Yelland."

"Really, Miss Yelland, Janet is *not* rude."

The noise and turmoil increased as the mistress rather foolishly argued with them. She realised that she ought not to have given in to them, but once begun, it was difficult to pull up, and so the lesson went on unsatisfactorily, until the mistress departed thankfully to a more congenial atmosphere.

The unregenerate Fourth chuckled, though Connie shook her head. "Not quite clever," she objected. "After all, she's only young."

"Yes, Grandmama," sang out Maureen.

"Well, let's try it on mademoiselle," suggested Ronnee. "She's quite old."

Unfortunately, Mlle. Henri arrived just at this moment, and she must have heard the remark.

"You should not talk when you are left alone," she admonished them in her careful English. "It should be a point of honneur viz,—with you."

"Sorry, Mademoiselle," apologised Connie for the form, and the French mistress was nodding graciously when echoes of the apology began to float from different parts of the room.

"Sorry, Mademoiselle."

"So sorry, Mademoiselle Henri."

"Oh, Mam'selle—sorry."

"Nous le regrettons, Mademoiselle."

"S'il vous plaît, Mademoiselle—"

The mistress held up her hand. "We will now finish being sorry, thank you. Ouvrez vos livres."

And the Fourth, their Spring Fever temporarily abated, settled down docilely enough to French, until Christine, happening to glance out of the window, saw something that made her scowl and bite her lip.

"Eh bien, Christine, you must attend." Mademoiselle sounded as if her patience were wearing thin.

Back flowed the Spring Fever into the veins of the Fourth, and Ronnee rushed into the fray.

"Oh, Mademoiselle, Christine *is* attending."

Mademoiselle's already pointed eyebrows disappeared like two little arrows into her hair.

"Comment!" she began, but by now the game was in full swing.

"She *is* attending, Mademoiselle."

"Oh, Mademoiselle, you *are* unkind!"

"Oh, poor Christine!" wailed Priscilla, and Sheila looked daggers across at her.

"Silly cuckoos!" whispered Christine crossly. "I wasn't attending," and Connie rose to her feet to try to bring the girls to their senses.

"Asseyez-vous," the French mistress hissed at her thinking that she was about to launch a fresh outburst of insubordination. Mlle Henri was not inclined, this morning to make allowances for the girls. Their remark about her age had been rude, and they were following it up with rudeness. She rose to her feet and waited for the whispering and giggling to subside.

"And now," she said at last, "since we 'ave silence instead of the so stupid chattering, I will tell you what you may do this afternoon, all of you." She then proceeded to give them a stiff dose of translation, to be handed to her when she came to preside over preparation that evening. She also gave them a much larger amount of preparation than usual. Maureen began tentatively to groan, in a heartbroken way, but the French mistress's eyes flickered at her with such fire in their black depths, that her groan petered out, and no one else had the courage to set up another. Mademoiselle did not give them her usual friendly smile as they left the class-room at midday break, but regarded them aloofly, as if they were interesting exhibits. And Christine, for whom the "show" had been staged, showed no gratitude for their championship. She had hardened suddenly into her old self, and walked on ahead of the girls.

"Oh, look, there's Mrs. Cameron!" whispered Janet as they passed a window. "Smashing, isn't she?"

Sheila knew now what was the matter with Christine. She looked quickly out of the window and received a surprise. Although the girls had told her that Mrs. Cameron was an old Grey-courtier, she had taken for granted that the lady belonged to many generations ago. But the person walking so gaily across the quad, was little more than a girl; certainly in her early twenties and pretty and elegant. Yes, elegant, that's what it was, Sheila told herself, as she took another peep. Mrs. Cameron was shorter and much more slender than Miss Meredith with whom she was walking, but even at this distance she seemed to sparkle with life.

Miss Meredith, walking more quickly than usual to keep up with her old pupil's dancing footsteps gave a sudden laugh.

"Isn't your husband ever tired out with your energy, Dolores, my dear?"

The brilliance of the girl's smile seemed to be reflected in the jewels at her throat, on her fingers and at her ears. Dolores Cameron *was* active; she was in love with life.

"Oh, John takes me in his stride," her voice trilled out gaily. "He's quiet himself and likes me to do the talking for us both. As for Joan, the little rascal, she can beat me any time."

"And talking of rascals, Dolores, brings me to what I intended to say before you distracted my thoughts. What are you going to do about your protégé?"

Some of the sparkle departed from Dolores' eyes. She looked baffled. "I wish I knew Miss Meredith. I do wish I knew. She dislikes me so heartily that I'm half scared to talk to her. I always say the wrong thing."

"Perhaps you are too kind to her."

"Oh, dear! Can one be too kind to a girl who has had such trouble? Miss Meredith, if you'd seen her—a forlorn little thing—sitting quietly in a corner of a crowded kitchen with absolute hopelessness in her eyes—mother dead—father in prison—no one in the world caring what became of her."

"Except my warm-hearted Dolores."

"I should say of course that the people who took her in cared what became of her," amended Dolores, not appearing to hear Miss Meredith's comment. "I understand that her mother had been rather trying, perhaps because of her health, and had quarrelled with their relations and friends. Her father made frantic efforts in the short time he had to get her taken care of, but as far as I know no one answered his appeals. Well, I rang up Daddy—"

"And how much did that cost you?" Miss Meredith asked with mock severity, for Dolores' father lived in America.

"Oh, quite a bit, I must say. Well, daddy got a friend in London to do all that was necessary, dispose of the house, and so on. I only acted as a go-between."

The first bell rang out, warning Greycourtiers, far and near, to hie them to the dining-hall.

"Well, Dolores, I only hope she'll justify your kindness," Miss Meredith observed, as they made their way together to lunch. "I really cannot consider keeping her here next year if she doesn't stop causing trouble."

"Oh, *please*, Miss Meredith."

"I won't do anything hastily, I promise you, but see what you can do to make her take a more sensible view of things."

Not an easy task to set oneself, thought Dolores as she made her way over to her ward after lunch. Christine shook hands politely, and answered all questions put to her, but she stood passively and made no attempt to sustain the conversation.

"Well, I've got the car," Mrs. Cameron said cheerfully. "What would you like—tea in the nearest town or tea at the George Inn here? They give you quite a good tea there I know."

"They give you quite a good tea here too," Christine answered flatly, "but anyway, I can't go out this afternoon. I've got a detention— all the Fourth have."

"You don't say!" Mrs. Cameron's eyes twinkled. "What have you been up to?"

"Oh—er," Christine shrugged, "I'm afraid you wouldn't understand."

"I'm quite sure I would! Still, if you don't want to discuss it—all right. How about some pocket-money?" Mrs. Cameron opened her bag as she spoke.

"I don't need any, thank you. I haven't touched the last you gave me."

Mrs. Cameron regarded her silently for a

moment, then she said gently, "Isn't that rather a pity? I know from experience that you're always wanting money for something or other here—don't forget I'm an old Courtier. I can see no reason why you shouldn't spend it."

And then Christine's temper, which she had kept so well under control just recently, flashed out, "Oh, no, you wouldn't," she snapped out, "I won't spend it anyway."

"Well, I say that is a foolish attitude to adopt."

"Oh, do you! Just because you are rich, you think you have the right to run everyone's lives. I hate everything about this place. You made me come, I had no choice. I'd much rather go back to the Peters. They understand me and I like being with them. So, well that's how I feel—" she trailed off rather lamely for Mrs. Cameron was regarding her very coolly.

"Well"— at last, and in a leisurely way, Dolores Cameron closed her bag and drew on her gloves—"while I am here, I may as well pay a few visits. You'd better get along to the DR, hadn't you?"

With a nod, she turned on her heel, and Christine was left rather nonplussed. She hadn't enjoyed the look in her visitor's eyes, and she hadn't expected to be left suddenly like that.

Dolores, two unusually bright spots burning on her cheeks, walked across to the Sanatorium where she received a friendly greeting from matron.

"You don't look as cheerful as usual, Dolores," she remarked. "Anything troubling you?"

Dolores grinned rather ruefully, and for the moment matron almost felt that the schoolgirl Dolores was back again.

"Christine's troubling me, Miss Wills."

"Oh, that little wretch! Well, I suppose I shouldn't have said that, but you ought not to have sent her here, you know. She's upset the form ever since she's been here. But I mustn't go on like this—it's only that the poor children haven't had an excellent, or whatever it is they get, for nearly a year now; no chance of it while she's about to let them down. Look," she added hurriedly, seeing Dolores so downcast. "I'm going across to River Cottage this afternoon. Why don't you come with me? You know Mrs. Solway will love to see you, and I've always found her a help in matters like this!"

Dolores' eyes lighted up. "Say, I'd like that! She was so good to us when we were here."

So, off they went in the car to River Cottage where lived Ursula Solway, beloved of many generations of Greycourtiers.

CHAPTER THIRTEEN

RIVER COTTAGE

"There she is!" exclaimed Dolores excitedly, as the car ran to a standstill at the little gate of River Cottage. Mrs. Solway was walking down the tiny path.

Matron laughed. "You're not in the least grown up, are you?"

"I'm grown up enough to have a husband and a child," Dolores told her with a pout. "I'm very hurt that you haven't mentioned them."

"Oh, my dear…" began Matron apologetically, but at that moment, the door of the car was pulled open and Dolores found herself folded in the arms of her old friend.

"My dear, grown-up, elegant little Dolores," exclaimed Mrs. Solway, holding the girl away from her and examining her with frank interest. "And married too! Every happiness, dear."

Dolores sighed happily. "You're the most satisfactory person I know. I've been longing to talk about it."

Mrs. Solway tucked her arm through that of

Dolores. "And so you shall, over a cup of tea. I want to know every detail, from how you first met him—though, of course he must be Mary's brother—right up to your marriage."

"This is just what I've been wanting," Dolores said contentedly. "Why didn't I come to you before?"

Matron followed them into the little house, an amused smile on her face—she was entirely out of the picture to-day. All through the meal Dolores chattered, mostly of course about her beloved John and Joan, but also of her experiences during the war and afterwards, and her two listeners were quite willing to be spellbound by their vivacious little friend. At last, the stream of conversation showed signs of running dry, and matron put in her word.

"You'd never dream I brought Dolores over here for a specific purpose," she said, smiling grimly. "Actually, she was in such depths of depression that I thought it would cheer her up. She seems, however, to have made a magnificent recovery!"

Dolores jumped. "Gracious! I completely forgot! I really came rushing over for advice just as I used to when I was at Greycourt. Help me, won't you please!" and matron and Mrs. Solway smiled at one another. This was indeed the old Dolores. "See here. I've adopted a kiddie who was—"

But at this moment, there was a loud ringing of bicycle bells and two Greycourt girls wheeled their bicycles past the window. It was Margaret, with another Sixth-former, Hilda Cartip. Hilda was not in the least fussy when with her own friends, and to Dolores, she seemed just another normal schoolgirl.

"I shall be sorry if we're late for tea," she remarked airily to her hostess. "Old Margaret had to get a puncture—she would! I suppose all the tea's gone?"

"You suppose wrongly," Mrs. Solway assured her, "and you'll find some more cakes in the kitchen. But first let me introduce you. Dolores, this is Margaret Rainer, the Captain, and Hilda Cartip the Vice-Captain. Girls, this is Mrs. Cameron, but you've seen her name on the Captain's board as Dolores Delvarro."

"Oh!" The two girls accorded Dolores all the homage due to her past greatness. "We know quite a lot about you," Margaret told her. "You didn't leave such an awfully long while ago."

"That's so," Dolores agreed, and her smile flashed as in former days. "It seems only yesterday to me. But it comes as a bit of a shock to find other Courtiers in possession. I thought River Cottage belonged to my particular set! Tell me what happens nowadays."

The girls were not shy—not many girls were by the time they had reached the Sixth, at Greycourt—and they regaled her with accounts of the school life, though at the same time they managed to eat a substantial tea. Dolores, in her turn, told them of some of the exploits of her days, and the time passed so quickly, that they had to rush off in the end. But Mrs. Solway had time for a few words with them before they went. "Special favour please, you most important persons," she begged. "Mrs. Cameron is worried about Christine—you know, Christine Barry? I don't know quite what the trouble is, but a little help from you might make all the difference. Will you?"

Margaret didn't answer as readily as Mrs. Solway had hoped for. She looked first rather doubtfully at Hilda, then said slowly, "I wish it had been any one else. You see, she's rather a difficult person to help."

"And as for me," Hilda spoke breathlessly, "I only seem to see her when she's doing something she oughtn't to be!"

"Well, you're a fine pair, I must say."

Margaret hastened to reassure her. "I'll keep an eye on her. I will really. And I won't let Hilda fuss over her."

"I like that!" Hilda was highly indignant.

"And I'm satisfied," Mrs. Solway told them. "She's safe in your hands."

"We'll have to cut across the field paths," Margaret said, as they mounted their bicycles and Mrs. Solway waved them out of sight before she returned to her guests. As usual, matron had her eye on the clock.

"I always have to rush off to the shops when I visit you Ursula. I simply must go to the chemist and he'll shut soon. Dolores, what about it? Do you want to go back yet?"

"No, she doesn't," answered Mrs. Solway for her. "She's staying with me as long as possible. I wish you hadn't fixed up to stay at the school, Dolores. It would have been lovely to have you here. Still, here you stay until you've absolutely got to go, and I won't have any argument."

Dolores chuckled. "You won't get any argument from me. I'm only too pleased to stay."

So matron went off shaking her head, and Dolores and her hostess settled down for a talk over old times. But after they had discussed Jill Winter, and Mary Cameron, and Doreen Welford and several other girls who had been regular visitors to River Cottage, Dolores once again began to look worried.

"Do you want to talk about it now?" Mrs. Solway asked gently.

Dolores managed a smile. "Haven't I always brought my troubles to River Cottage? Of course I want to talk about it."

"Then I shall love to listen," and Mrs. Solway picked up her knitting.

"I'm afraid I made a big mistake in taking

charge of Christine," Dolores began. "I suppose it was a nerve for any one as young as I am to have attempted such a thing."

"Age has nothing to do with it," Mrs. Solway put in. "There are people of fifty who can't even make a decision, let alone take a definite step. Go on dear."

Two unexpected tears ran down Dolores' face.

"I—she doesn't like it at Greycourt—hates it —won't spend the money I give her. Matron tells me she annoys the girls and spoils her form's chances of getting honours. Christine told me definitely that she'd rather go back to that slum where the people understood her."

"Then why not let her?" Mrs. Solway asked. Dolores looked at her in amazement. "Send her back to that awful overcrowded house? She didn't belong there, you know, she—she—" But it was no use: Dolores found she couldn't continue.

"I think I know most of her history," said her old friend soothingly. "You heard about her at your welfare centre and went along to the house to see if you could help. Poor people, who already were crowded in a small house, had taken her in, in the goodness of their hearts, and because they were so sorry for her, they let her do exactly as she pleased. But as soon as you saw the conditions in which she was living, you appealed to your father, who furnished the necessary funds and pulled strings, and between you, you got her into Greycourt. Well everybody at Greycourt tried to make life so pleasant for her, that she speedily recovered from the shock and sorrow, and developed a swelled head instead. Schoolgirls wouldn't stand for that in any one, and dealt with her drastically. She wouldn't learn her lesson, but preferred to keep the centre of the stage by foul means when fair ones failed. Isn't that the case?"

"In a nutshell," Dolores said admiringly. "What shall I do?"

"Give her her wish. She thinks, or pretends to think, that she has been torn away from people who understand her. All right. Let her go back to them."

"Oh, I couldn't. She's a troublesome kid, I know, but she isn't the same as they are, truly. They are decent hard-working folk, but they themselves were glad that she was getting a chance to be with people of her own sort. They told me so."

"Well, I still say let her go back." Mrs. Solway was putting away her work as she spoke. "Not for good, of course, but for long enough to make her realise what it would be like to live with them altogether. I think she'll want to come back to Greycourt, but if she still doesn't, well you'll have to do what you can for her in some other way. Try it Dolores."

Her visitor sighed with relief. "I knew you'd help me. Yes, at least we can try it, though I'm sure she'll hate it after Greycourt."

And now it was time to say an affectionate good-bye to the Lady of River Cottage and to hurry back to Greycourt, where she was having supper privately with Janet Faulkner, an old classmate of hers, who was now a Junior Mistress at the school. And later, when Dolores had fallen asleep after an exciting day, Christine was thinking, "Hm! Pretends she's so friendly, and can't even take the trouble to say good-bye before she goes." With which sweet and reasonable thought, Christine also closed her eyes in sleep.

CHAPTER FOURTEEN

OFF TO LONDON

Christine, upon reflection, was a little worried over her short meeting with Mrs. Cameron, especially as she had heard nothing further. Probably she was going to be taken at her word and sent away from Greycourt. It was so unlike Mrs. Cameron to leave her in suspense that she was a little uneasy, and more than a little irritable.

For the first time, she and Priscilla had a quarrel. It was about a very trivial matter. Priscilla was bouncing a ball as they were making their way over to the playing fields, and it flew sideways, striking Christine on the chin. With a grunt of irritation, Christine picked it up and flung it with all her force, back into the quadrangle.

"What d'you do that for, you chump!" demanded Priscilla.

"Because I don't intend to have any more bangs on the chin. That's why."

"Oh, I'm sorry. I couldn't help it."

"Well, you won't get the chance to do it again.

You wouldn't like it if it had hit you."

"I've said sorry, haven't I? Can't you let it drop now?"

"Only too glad, if you've finished acting like a fathead."

Priscilla stopped dead in her tracks. "Look here, Christine Barry," she blazed out. "I've had just about enough of you. You're the rudest, worst-tempered girl I've ever met. I'm not going to have anything more to do with you." And she flung herself off in a great rage.

Christine gave another grunt. "That didn't last long," she remarked. "You'll be the next, Sheila."

Sheila smiled. "I hope not," she said in her sincere way. "I should miss you now."

And straightway the world became less upside down for her turbulent little friend. Sheila meant what she said. Christine, in spite of her rudeness and unpredictable temper, was a most interesting person to have for a friend. Sheila knew, without knowing how she knew, that Christine could become a powerful influence for good in the school. She didn't know how to help her, but at least she could stand her friend, whatever happened, and this she was resolved to do.

Contrary to Christine's ideas, Mrs. Cameron had had her very much in mind, and was engaged in active business on her account, and

before long arrangements were being made for
Christine's return to her friends. Although there
was still a fortnight to go before the Easter
holidays, Doctor Atkinson agreed that the girl
was in need of immediate change of environment.
He had expressed this opinion to matron already,
and now was prepared to recommend this change
at once.

The next step was to interview Mrs. Peters
and a trip up to town was necessary for that.
Dolores had some difficulty in convincing the
good hard-working woman that Christine really
did want to stay at her home.

"Why, she must be mad!" Mrs. Peters exclaimed.
"Lovely country it is down there, my daughter
tells me, and look at this! We've been trying to
get another place for months."

"Well, that's how things are," Dolores explained. "And since she's had a bad cold, and is
rather pulled down, the doctor recommends that
she doesn't wait till the Easter holidays. The
point is, do you feel you can be bothered with
her?"

"She wasn't any bother before, Miss," said
Mrs. Peters, who had known Dolores before she
was married. "I'm used to girls—should be,
with four of my own. Yes, if Mr. Peters is
agreeable, she's welcome to all we've got here
for your sake. You've been very good to us."

"Oh, thank you, and of course I won't let you

stand any of the expense—no, please don't let's talk about that part of it. Actually, I want you to help me. I know you'll be kind to her, but I want you to let her live as one of the family. Don't treat her as a guest."

Mrs. Peters nodded reassuringly. "I get your meaning, Miss. Just treat her as I would one of my own children, eh?"

"Oh, yes, that's what I want."

"Poor little soul. Don't you worry, Miss. You've done all you could."

Mr. Peters raised no objection to the plan, since he supposed he wouldn't see much of Christine anyway, and Dolores heaved a sigh of relief as she went off to her own family.

"I'll never try to manage anyone else's business again," she thought, and then laughed aloud. "I wonder how many times I've said that before!"

At Greycourt, Margaret and Hilda attempted to carry out the promise made to Mrs. Solway, but as they had predicted, Christine wasn't easy to help. She was polite and evasive with Margaret, and openly rude to Hilda, much to the delight of the bright spirits of the Fourth who hadn't much patience with Hilda either.

"I can't think why Hilda doesn't report her," chuckled Ronnee one afternoon. "If any of us said half as much as the pest, we'd be sent to Merry. She never is sent up, is she, Sheila?"

"If you mean Christine—no," Sheila replied.

"Oh, beg pardon, Shee!" apologised Ronnee.

"As a matter of fact she's been much more bearable since you've been back," Janet told her. "I've liked her quite a bit this term."

Sheila smiled her friendliest. "That's good. I think she'll settle down soon now. She's a grand person really."

"Well, she certainly keeps us alive."

At this juncture Christine walked into the room, looking a little dazed. There was a momentary silence, as there always is, when the person under discussion appears unexpectedly, and her mouth curved into a sarcastic smile.

"Don't let me interrupt you. You *were* talking about me—weren't you?"

"Yes," Connie said directly. "But only in a nice way. You wouldn't have minded."

Christine looked up, then down again.

"Well, I shan't bother you much longer," she mumbled. "I'm going back to nay friends in London."

This was indeed a sensation.

"Why? What have you done?"

"Who's making you?"

"Oh, Christine!" This from Sheila, who simply couldn't help sounding reproachful.

Christine had recovered her self-assurance by now. She waved a letter in her hand. "I've just had this from Mrs. Cameron. She's arranged it. I—I asked her to," she added defiantly.

"Well, if you want to go—" began Maureen.

"Oh, but I do!" The idea was growing upon Christine and she was becoming excited at the thought of a change from school life. "It's supposed to be just till the end of the Easter holidays, but I expect they'll let me stay altogether if I ask. Good-bye," she said abruptly and turned on her heel, but at the door she paused and said, "You're being very nice, but really you'll be glad if I go."

Waving aside murmurs of dissent, she closed the door behind her, and then discovered that Sheila was at her side.

"Oh, you made me jump!" she exclaimed, with a forced laugh. "Are you going to help me to pack?"

"If you like. When are you going?"

"To-morrow morning, I think."

There was silence as they walked to the dormitory. Christine looked sideways at her friend once or twice, but Sheila could not, or would not, talk. In the dormitory matron had placed two suitcases in readiness, and Christine, opening her chest of drawers, began methodically to pack.

"Well, is there anything I can do?" asked Sheila at last."

"You—you might look less disapproving to begin with," Christine told her. "After all, I've always said this was what I wanted."

"Look here, Sheila." Christine tried to carry

off the situation with a show of anger. "Are you trying to spoil things for me? Why don't you say what's the matter?"

"Nothing's the matter," Sheila said, with an effort. "I don't want to spoil your fun. It's—it's just that—well, I can't help being rather disappointed."

Christine tossed her head. "Well, I can't help that, can I? You've expected too much of me. The girls told you what I was like, but you wouldn't believe them. Now you know it's true."

"I don't know what you are talking about," Sheila said dully. "I only know that you've asked to go away and you're going. Doesn't seem a very friendly thing to have done, does it?"

"No, it—it doesn't," Christine agreed. "I didn't realise it before though. Still—" she hesitated, for Sheila looked as if she were about to cry. They both folded garments, and packed as they had been taught to do, and after a while Sheila was herself again.

"Is this to go in?" she asked, holding up a blotter. "No? Well, I'll put it at the side here. I do hope you are going to have a happy time, Christine."

"Oh, I'm sure to," Christine said jauntily. "I'll write and tell you all about it. You'll write to me, won't you?"

"Of course I will."

Matron came in then and there was no more private conversation. Christine could hardly sleep that night for excitement, and it was with barely concealed glee that she bade Sheila good-bye the next morning.

Free! Free! Free! The train seemed to keep pace with her thoughts, as it covered the miles of Sussex country, but Christine had no eyes for the beauty of the scenery. She was looking forward to a town street, with plenty of people in it, and a small house where she could do as she pleased and not be bound by rules. Oh, hurry up, train! she was thinking; let's get there, let's get there!

Mrs. Cameron met her at Victoria Station and took her to lunch in a West-End store. This was exciting enough in itself, and Christine unbent sufficiently to say, "Thank you very much, Mrs. Cameron, for letting me go to the Peters."

"Think nothing of it," Dolores told her kindly. "You haven't been very well. The change will do you good."

"I hope I stay for good," Christine rejoined, with a flash of her old spirit. "I don't want to go back."

Dolores did not answer that, and Christine had the grace to say, "I didn't mean to be rude to you," which was accepted with a quizzical smile. They were on the final stage of the journey by then and Christine was about to have her wish fulfilled. The car drew up in front of the little house, in a shabby suburb of London, and Mrs. Peters opened the door to them herself.

From the moment that she entered that house Christine seemed a different girl. She smiled delightedly and her eyes were like stars. Dolores had never seen her so happy, and she was able to leave them all without further misgivings.

CHAPTER FIFTEEN

THE FOLLOWING WEEK

"I'm sick of this term," declared Ronnee. "I'll be very glad when it's Easter."

"Boo-Hoo-Hoo-Hoo! What's the matter, lambie love?" jeered Maureen. "Did she get an imposition then."

"Pity *you* haven't got to do it; you wouldn't be quite so cheerful then. Why on earth they had to do away with conduct marks, I don't know."

"Oh, stop grumbling, and get it over."

"If anyone asked for it this morning, you did," Connie said in her direct way. "I wondered why Miss Masterson didn't speak to you before."

"Well, I like that! I'm not taking the pest's place by any chance, am I?"

Connie shook her head. She was unusually serious. "I'm not at all sure now that she was wholly to blame for—"

But several girls protested at that, and Connie added, "Well, we have had a week without her, and what have we to show for it?"

"Peace and quiet," growled Janet.

"But we haven't—that's just it!" Poor Connie was getting hotter and more uncomfortable as she went on. "I know you'll think me a kill-joy, but honestly I think we've shown up pretty badly. We can't blame Christine for the silly things that have happened this week. Yes, you know what I mean," and she looked round first at Maureen, who had taken out and hidden the electric bulb from Hilda's cubicle, and was now grinning at the remembrance of the disturbance; then at Ronnee, who had put the wireless on so loudly that it brought a mistress on the scene, with a lecture for them all—Ronnee placed her finger to her cheek and gazed pensively out of the window; then at Priscilla, who, on being dared to do so, had opened the grand piano in Big Hall, and had played a dance tune to the delight of her Fourth Form confederates, and the horror of Margaret, who was in the act of conducting the captain of a neighbouring school around. Even now Priscilla couldn't see anything funny about her interview with Margaret afterwards and she frowned as she met Connie's eyes.

"And while we are on the subject," Sheila put in, "we may as well admit it's pretty low down to rag a mistress as we did."

"Oh, don't be so superior, Sheila," Maureen said, looking annoyed. "And don't say 'we'—you weren't in it."

"Sorry," Sheila answered flatly.

"Now," Connie spoke determinedly, "I've said what I wanted to say, and we'll drop it, shall we?" The girls sighed with relief and Ronnee burst out laughing. "Pity Christine isn't here to say something outrageously rude."

They scattered then—Ronnee to pay the penalty of her waywardness, none the worse for a little plain speaking, and the others to the playing fields, there to wander about desultorily, for the ground still was wet and soggy. But Sheila went upstairs to the library. She was lonely—more lonely than she had ever been before and she missed Christine very much. After her friend had gone, Sheila had reproached herself for her lack of enthusiasm, and had written as soon as she could, telling Christine every scrap of news that she could gather. Now everything seemed stale and unprofitable. Examinations were over, leaving them all rather tired and fractious. The winter had been severe and the roads still were bad for walking. Sheila caught sight of her reflection in a mirror, and smiled involuntarily. "Gracious! What a morbid person I'm becoming!" she thought, and squared her shoulders. "No wonder the girls called me superior. This *won't* do! You thought you were going to make all the difference to Christine, didn't you?" she said to herself in the glass. "Well, perhaps another time you won't think you're so wonderful. Why should you succeed where all the others failed?" But she covered her eyes with her hands all the same, and wished with all her heart that Christine would come back....

And then she became conscious of a gentle touch on her shoulder and, looking up guiltily, she saw Margaret.

"Can I help?" the head girl asked in her friendly way. "Never mind. I think I know what it is," she went on as Sheila made an attempt to answer, and failed. "Christine, isn't it?"

Sheila nodded, still speechless, though she gave Margaret a watery smile.

"Well, let's see what we can do about it," the older girl said practically. "She's only having an extended holiday, isn't she? Aren't you likely to see her during the holidays?"

"No, I don't think so, Margaret. I—I don't think she would want to come to my home and there wouldn't be room for visitors in the house she's in."

"I see. Well, don't make it worse by fretting over it. The time will soon go, and she'll be back again before you know where you are."

"Not if she can help it!" Sheila returned, with her first show of spirit. "She's hoping to persuade Mrs. Cameron to let her leave."

"Strange!" Margaret looked rather troubled. "She's always been a little rebel, but I wonder if we've failed in any way, too?" She regarded

Sheila thoughtfully for a moment or two, then shook her head and smiled. "Well, this won't do any good. Look, if you're not doing anything particularly, will you go across to the hotel and pick up some books for me? Father and mother are taking me out for a spell, and probably they'll drop me here on the way back, so I'd be glad if the books were here."

"Yes, of course I'd love to, Margaret."

"Thanks. You'll have to take someone with you, and afterwards you may stay out till tea-time. Who'll it be?" asked Margaret, who was scribbling a permit.

"Priscilla. I'm sure she'd like to come."

"Right!" Margaret handed the paper over. "And Sheila, we'll both believe that Christine is coming back, see? When she returns, I'll try to help. That make it better?"

"Very much!" Sheila smiled gratefully at the head girl. "Thank you ever so much, Margaret."

Priscilla was delighted to have a break from school, and the two girls made their way down to the village where stood the comfortable old hotel, facing the village green. They collected Margaret's books, and then set out for a short walk. Their spirits revived as the fresh air flowed into their lungs and soon they were laughing and talking and making plans for Christine's return.

They arrived back at school just as the outside

bell was ringing for tea, and they amazed the rest of the Fourth by their appetites. And to complete a happy afternoon, Sheila found a letter from Christine awaiting her in the letter-rack.

"A-ha!" Priscilla grinned, as Sheila tore open the letter in haste. "Here we go again!"

Sheila glanced up smiling, though she had not heard the remark, and then continued reading her letter.

"...I've been here a week and it has been a really wonderful week. I don't think I realised how much I hated being away at school until I came away from it. When I look round this cosy little kitchen, with the tea things all ready for when Dolly comes in from school, I feel ever so sorry for you all, having to go over to that huge dining-hall, with its rows and rows of polished tables—just like prison! I know my address doesn't sound as imposing as Greycourt, Greatoaks, Sussex, or White Lodge, Fairfield, Hants., but to me it spells Freedom Hall, Utopia."

Sheila laughed—it was almost like Christine talking in her old arrogant way.

"They don't fuss round or worry me, and I stay in bed as late as I like in the morning. I've been to the pictures twice already and we go to bed just when we fancy. No bells ringing and wild scurryings along corridors. Even when we're in bed, we read just as long as we want to, and then I tell them of things that have happened at Greycourt, and they just lap it up. The freedom of it all is marvellous! I know you don't agree with me, but that's because you've always been used to restrictions. I don't like them!

I expect you'd turn your aristocratic nose up at conditions here, but they don't worry me. I haven't been along yet to the place I used to live in. Somehow I can't. Mrs. Peters offered to come with me to call on old neighbours. She has some weird notion that they would be 'Better For Me' than her own family. I wish people would believe me when I say I know what I want. Still, I must say Mrs. Peters dropped the subject when she found I didn't like it.

I hope you will have a decent holiday, Sheila. At least, it will be more peaceful than the last. Still, I did warn you, though I'm sorry I upset things at the party. There! I don't often apologise, do I? It must be the effect of my new-found happiness. I hope I'll never have to go back to Greycourt. Perhaps I can convince Mrs. Cameron if she condescends to visit me. They almost worship her in these parts; she does seem to have done a lot for them. But I haven't seen much of her this year. The last time she came to Greycourt she didn't even bother to say 'good-bye' when she left!

It was quite a thrill to get your letter, Sheila, and to hear all the school news. Yes, of course I'll like to hear from Priscilla—the silly cuckoo!

Please write to me again if you can, and I'll let you know what happens here.

CHRISTINE."

Sheila folded the letter. "She wants you to write, Pris," she said, and added excitedly, "and I feel sure, somehow, that she'll want to come back to school."

CHAPTER SIXTEEN

LIFE AT PETERS'

Christine enjoyed her first week of holiday. It was fun to help Mrs. Peters in the house, and to buy things in the shops for her; thrilling to be taken to the cinema twice in a few days. Best of all, she enjoyed entertaining an admiring audience formed of the two Peters schoolgirls. Now and again she would pause and wonder what they were doing at Greycourt, especially Sheila and the Fourth, but she had too much to distract her, to allow her to dwell on the wisdom of coming away. Nevertheless, she was overwhelmingly glad when she saw Sheila's familiar writing on the envelope which Mrs. Peters brought in to her. Eagerly she tore it open and read the news that Sheila had gathered so painstakingly. Dear Sheila—how near and real she made all the details of school life. Christine could visualise them all—it made it seem somehow as if she hadn't left before the end of term after all. And Priscilla wanted to write to her. Fancy! She had not thought that Pris would

care that much. She looked up smiling and
caught Mrs. Peters' eye.

"Enjoying it?" asked that comfortable matron
who was making a pudding.

Christine nodded happily. "Yes, it's nice to hear
about it when you're away from it. Must be
awful there, this weather!" She snuggled contentedly near the kitchen fire and watched Mrs.
Peters who was working away so placidly.
Presently, however, she was reading her letter
again, and Mrs. Peters smiled to herself.

"Isn't there anything I can do to help you?"
Christine said after a little while. "I feel so lazy
sitting here doing nothing."

"Why, my dear, you've done quite a lot—
helped me with the beds and done the dusting.
You're supposed to be getting over illness. Take
it easily now, there's nothing more to be done,"
and Mrs. Peters gave her a reassuring smile as
her capable hands kneaded the dough. But
Christine wasn't patient enough to sit still for
long, and presently she made another request.
"Would you mind if I went out and got some
paper and ink?"

"Of course I wouldn't my dear—you run
along. The only thing is, be careful of the traffic.
There have been a good many accidents lately
what with the bad weather and that."

So Christine put on her thick coat and went out
walking. After she had bought her writing

materials, she made her way over to the small recreation ground which served the district. Here she saw two girls playing tennis, and Christine, who was a good player herself, watched the game with some enjoyment. One of the girls was tall and thin and had an imperious air about her. "Maria!" she would call sharply if her opponent dared to look away for a moment. The girl called Maria, was plump and pleasant-looking and wore her hair in two flaxen plaits around her head. Although she didn't seem to have her heart in this game, it was easy to see that she was an expert tennis player. Her service was superb and her timing almost uncannily accurate. Christine sighed regretfully as she left them still playing, but she determined to bring her racquet in future and try to get a few games in.

It was time for midday dinner when she got back, and Mrs. Peters had her hands full, for the girls were hungry and noisy and wanting to play, but as soon as the house was quiet again, Christine sat down and wrote to Sheila. Somehow, she felt more settled now that she was in contact with her school friends.

The next week began happily enough and the Fourth would not have known Christine, as, with a huge apron around her, she washed up the breakfast things at the scullery sink, singing away at the top of her voice. But as the days went on, she began to find time hanging heavily on her hands, though she consoled herself with the thought that the girls would soon be on holiday, and they could make plans.

There was great jubilation when they broke up for the Easter holiday.

"Mum, can we go to the Zoo next week?" Dolly wanted to know.

"No, let's go on a boat," from Louise.

"Can Sally come in to tea with us, Mum?" Sally was their special chum.

"We'll have to see," was all that their mother would promise. "If you don't behave yourselves, it'll be Bedfordshire for the lot of you."

This was hailed as a great joke, which they insisted on sharing with their father when he came in that evening and during the romp which followed, Christine slipped upstairs and mended a pair of stockings.

On the following Monday, Mrs. Peters packed huge lunches for them and gave them their bus fares, and they set off for a Surrey common. Christine, who had missed the open spaces around Greycourt, was looking forward tremendously to a good blow of air and she hoped they would be able to get plenty of exercise in too—there was a ball in her pocket for that purpose.

The first set-back, as far as she was concerned, was when they were hailed by Sally King, who stood in a doorway holding a baby in her arms.

"Where are you going?" she called over to them

and when they told her, she rushed across the road regardless of the traffic. "I'll come too. Let me come with you."

The Peters girls looked at each other in perplexity. Sally was their friend and they had no objection to her coming, but the baby was quite a different proposition. They were afraid of getting into trouble.

"What about Sylvia?" enquired Dolly dubiously.

"Oh, she'll be all right. I've got her food for to-day. Don't you worry."

Christine was horrified. "Of course you can't bring her," she said sharply, "don't be ridiculous."

This was the worst thing she could have said. Louise and Dolly might have doubts themselves, but they certainly were not going to have their friend criticised by this girl.

"You mind your own business! 'Course she can come. Come on Sally."

"Half a minute, I'll wrap her up. You go on and I'll catch you up at the bus stop." And Sally, who had plenty of common sense, was left behind to make the necessary preparations. Like many children whose parents both went out to work she had learned early to look after domestic affairs. So she left a note to say where she had gone, put together the baby's food expertly and packed some lunch for herself. She took some money from the communal fund, locked up the house and set off to join the girls.

Dolly had tried to make up to Christine for their outburst.

"You'll like Sally," she told her, "she's ever so good at telling stories and things."

"Really!" was Christine's curt response.

Dolly looked disappointed. "Oh, I s'pose you're going to tell Mum. I do think you're mean!"

"I don't tell tales," Christine returned loftily. "Do let's forget about it. I was only worried about the baby."

"She'll be all right. Sally's looked after her ever since she was born. Oh, here is Sally," as their friend hurried up to them with the baby on one arm and a large bag on the other.

"Look at Sylvia!" she crowed. "She knows she's going 'tats' doesn't she? She's been as good as gold all the while I've been getting ready. Did I ever tell you about—"

She regaled them with a story about the baby until the bus came along, when with much noise and laughter they scrambled on and then sorted themselves and their belongings out. The three friends chattered excitedly and amused the other passengers, but Christine hated the publicity, though she tried not to show it. Gradually, her silence had an effect on the others, and they began to show off for her benefit. This was intolerable, and Christine, who had plenty of courage, decided that she must take some sort of action.

"May I hold the baby," she enquired mildly.

Sally was so surprised, that she handed the child over without a word, though usually she was not disposed to grant this privilege. The three girls all waited for Sylvia to begin crying, for Christine held her awkwardly. But the baby did not cry. Instead, she looked up questioningly at her new nurse, then put out her little hand and touched the girl's face. For the rest of that journey, Christine was quite oblivious of the others. She and the baby were watching each other and evidently finding the occupation of absorbing interest.

Sally took over again when they alighted from the bus, and when the baby began to protest, she gave her a tap on the hand, much to Christine's indignation. They walked and dawdled until they came to a suitable spot, though Christine considered that they were much too near the road. Sally however with her usual common sense, decreed that the ground was still too wet to venture farther in, so they rested on a wooden bench, read the paper books and ate the fruit which the resourceful Sally had brought along. That young woman took advantage of the next few minutes of quietness to give the baby her milky food, but she was soon in demand again for a story. This time she launched forth into a description of a dance she had attended. Christine's thoughts wandered, rather far away, to Greycourt, where the girls would be tumbling downstairs at present to wash their hands before lunch. Hilda probably would fuss along and scold; Margaret would smile if she met them. The Fourth were either highly indignant over some injustice, or giggling because…

Christine pulled herself up and listened determinedly to Sally.

"He said, 'Do you go out to work?' and I said, 'Oh, yes, I'm a shorthand typist,' but— I don't think he believed me."

"Shall we have a game?" Christine asked taking out her ball. They all agreed, and while one held Sylvia, the others ran about with a great deal of shrieking. But now the rain which had been threatening for some time, began to fall in earnest and soon they were very wet, for no bus was available and the trees were not leafy enough to shelter them. Sylvia was the only completely dry one among them, for Sally took off her own coat and wrapped it around her.

They arrived home later that afternoon in a sorry plight and received a good scolding from Mrs. Peters, which was her way of showing how worried she had been. She sent Christine upstairs at once for a hot bath and made her own girls have a good dry-off in front of the fire, and soon they were sitting down to a high tea of sausages, toast and cakes. They were all pleasantly tired and quite willing to go to bed when the

time came, and they woke up the next day none
the worse for their wetting. Poor Sally was not
so fortunate. After giving the baby her food,
and putting her to bed, Sally had prepared the
evening meal for her parents, and had not
troubled to change her wet clothes. In consequence, when the three girls came in from the
cinema the next afternoon, they found little
Sylvia presiding over the kitchen, with many
gurgles and chuckles.

"Yes," Mrs. Peters told them as they exclaimed.
"Sylvia will stay here the next few days and her
mother will call for her in the evenings. Bless
her little heart, she's quite happy! Sally went
and caught cold and they've had to have the
doctor to her. You'll all have to take your turn
at looking after her. I've got me hands full."

But Sylvia in her small imperious way chose
Christine for her handmaid, and Christine was
delighted to receive this signal mark of favour.
With a sigh of relief, the girls left her to it for
they had had more than enough of minding
other people's babies in their time, and it became
the recognised thing that Christine took charge
of the baby. The holiday was passing unevent-
fully—indeed, if it had not been for Sylvia, who
caused her several bad patches of worry, Christine
would have said that the time dragged at this
period, but she consoled herself with the thought
that at least she was free from school life.

Then one day, Flo came home on holiday from Greycourt, and everything seemed to alter. She was sitting in the cosy little kitchen taking up all the fire, and talking to her sisters when Christine came upon her suddenly one afternoon.

"Yes, it's fine to be 'ome for a bit, kids, though it all seems smaller'n when I went away. That old school's such a whacking great place. Coo, kippers! That's the stuff, Mum. I haven't 'ad a kipper for tea since I don't know when."

"Draw up then and have your fill," chuckled her mother. "You always were a one for kippers. Oh, do you see who's here?" She indicated Christine whom she had just noticed.

Flo had seen her from the first but had given no sign of it. Now she nodded familiarly as she sat down to her tea.

"How do? Bin enjoying yourself?"

"Y-yes, thank you." Christine was rather nervous remembering their last meeting. "How's everybody at Greycourt?"

"How should I know? I'm only one of the servants."

"Flo!" murmured her mother, sensing that something was wrong, but not knowing quite what to do about it.

"It's all right, Mum. Pass the bread and butter, Dolly. I've got an appetite like an 'orse."

The conversation became general and Christine was able to pull herself together. "I'll never ask her anything again," she thought, with a flash of her old spirit, and as soon as she could, she began to get Sylvia ready to go home. Mrs. Peters came to her aid.

"Going to take her home yourself, dear? That's right. You won't mind sharing with the two girls while Flo's home will you? Their room's bigger than hers. I'll move your bed for you."

"N-no, of course not—thank you very much," she spoke confusedly and got herself and Sylvia out as quickly as possible.

Mr. Peters was in when she returned. He was making a great fuss of Flo and laughing up-roariously at her stories, but he gave his chair to Christine when she came into the kitchen, and he sat on the table. She didn't like to make a fuss, but, after this, she contrived while Flo was home to keep out of the little kitchen as much as possible, and this was made easier for her because by this time she had met Maria.

CHAPTER SEVENTEEN

NOT SO ROSY

Christine took Sylvia out as early as she could on the morning following Flo's homecoming. She wanted to get away before Flo came down to breakfast, and she wanted to read her letter in peace. Fortunately, it was fine, and she made her way over to the recreation ground. She played with Sylvia until that young lady showed signs of drowsiness, and then opened her letter.

"Dear Chris," Sheila had written, "I always think of you as Chris, so just smooth down your feathers and don't get cross. I hope you've been able to get out more than we have. The weather has been simply appalling, and we are all depressed and short-tempered with each other. Never mind, it will soon be time to go back to Greycourt and the nicer terms. I love old Greycourt in the summer—lessons out of doors—tennis—rambles. And for some reason—ridiculous, I suppose—I'm looking forward very much to meeting a certain Christine Barry!

"Your Mrs. Peters sounds a dear. I was telling

mother and Julie about the way you live—they were very interested. Poor Sally, I hope she's better. I'm not going to write a long letter—am looking forward to seeing you on the 23rd, but here's a letter Priscilla asked me to send on to you."

Priscilla's letter ran, "Hullo, there, stranger! It seems ages since I saw you. Did you know we all got into rows as soon as you departed? Ronnee for cheek, Maureen with old fussy Hilda, and I had a 'brief encounter' with Margaret! I take a very poor view of Margaret when she's in a paddy. You should have heard her—not nice at all! It was really rather disconcerting to find that we're all, more or less, villains. You've lost ground and you'll have to fight if you want to get back your position as villain-in-chief! The other day—"

Bang! Sylvia woke suddenly, and threw out her rattle, catching Christine smartly on the hand with it. Still smiling at Priscilla's nonsense, Christine gave it back to the child, who promptly threw it out again. Several times was her rattle returned with great patience, but Sylvia seemed to feel that she wasn't receiving the usual attention from her devoted attendant. With a prodigious effort, she flung the rattle beyond Christine and it fell into the lap of the other occupant of the seat—a girl with a pretty silk square tied round her head. This girl obligingly returned the rattle to its owner but not before Christine had noticed that she had been crying. Christine caught the rattle the next time the baby tried the trick, and was treated to a howl of rage from her charge, who indicated in unmistakable baby language what were her commands in the game.

"Oh, let her, please," the other girl said huskily. "I have nothing else to do."

"Er—all right then, if you don't mind," Christine said rather dubiously, but relieved to get back to her letter once more. She was grinning with enjoyment of the tale of the Fourth's escapades, when suddenly, the girl at the end of the seat dropped her head on her hands and burst into a torrent of weeping. Christine sat petrified. She had never seen unrestrained grief like this. After an interval the weeping subsided and the girl glanced sideways and murmured, "'Scuse me."

"Er—is there anything I can do?" Christine asked awkwardly.

The girl looked up, then turned her head away quickly. "No, no, I don't sink so, thank you."

Evidently a foreigner! Something like compassion awoke within Christine's hardened little heart. "Well, just tell me anyway," she said coaxingly. "I can't help with money, but sometimes it helps to talk."

"Oh, I have enough money for to live—I

mean—to live comfortably, sank you, but—"

But here Sylvia thought it time to remind them of her presence, and it was some time before the girl was able to tell her story.

She was Swiss, and her name was Maria Werterhof. She had been employed in an office at home, but had wanted to improve her knowledge of English, as already she could speak French, Italian and German. So she had applied to come to England as a domestic servant in order that she should speak English daily. Alas, it had not occurred to her that a mistress would hardly spend much time in conversation with a cook, and in her own particular house, the mistress did not speak to her directly about the meals, but delegated that duty to the nurse. Thus, although she had a comfortable home, and a fair amount of free time, the girl rarely spoke to anyone, for the woman who came in daily had a great contempt for foreigners, and the loneliness was eating into her heart.... Just then her head scarf fell back, revealing her luxuriant fair hair arranged in plaits.

"Haven't I seen you playing tennis with a tall girl?" exclaimed Christine suddenly.

Maria nodded. "She is the daughter. She has gone away for Easter, and anyway, her mother now says it is not right for her to go out with me." Her tears were flowing again and Christine felt a little impatient.

"Well, look here," she said, "if you care to, we could play tennis together whenever you like and I'll talk English to you. Are you allowed to come out fairly often?"

"Whenever the lady is away, or out to lunch, I may come out in the mornings. I must always be in at night to cook dinner—every night except Wednesday, when I go to the Commercial Institute for English."

"Well, I'd love to get some tennis practice in and you play a marvellous game, so I'll come along each morning in case you are here, and you can write out different bits in English—letter and so on, if you like, and I'll correct them for you as well as talk to you. Like that?"

"Oh, *yes*! That will be so good. I sank you— th-ank you so very much."

Christine felt quite excited at the prospect of tennis practice and in her restored good humour even made an attempt to placate Flo. Her good intentions were frustrated at the outset however. Flo just would not take any notice of her and had evidently aired her grievance, for Dolly and Louise were very much on their dignity. Still, Christine refused to be "downed" so easily.

"Shall we go out somewhere this afternoon?" she ventured to say to Dolly.

"I *am* going out," that damsel replied with a toss of her head. "My sister is taking us to the pictures."

"Yes, and to-morrow we're going to the Zoo," chimed in Louise impressively.

"That's good," Christine rejoined, as heartily as she could. "I hope you'll enjoy yourselves."

"'Course we will. P'raps you can find someone else to go out with."

"Oh, I shall be busy." Christine relapsed into curtness again. "I've letters to write."

"Coo! Fancy writing letters when you're on your holidays! Oo! And you can't have Sylvia any longer either, 'cos Sally's better."

But Flo called them into the scullery to wash their faces and the three of them went off to the pictures. Christine sat writing to Priscilla until Mrs. Peters bustled into the kitchen.

"I'm always glad when that meal is cleared away," she said, giving the fire a poke and pulling her chair forward. "There's a bit of breathing space before I start again. What have you been doing with yourself, my dear?"

Christine launched forth into the story about Maria, but didn't find Mrs. Peters as understanding as usual.

"I expect she's all right," that lady said, shaking her head at the same time, "but you have to be careful of people you meet like that. I don't hold with folks who throw up good jobs. Why don't they stay where they are well off?"

"She's got to remain here for a year anyway," pleaded Christine. "You'd feel sorry for her."

"I'm going to see her," Mrs. Peters said grimly. "I'll come along with you to-morrow morning and see what I think of her."

And in spite of all Christine's protests that is what she did, and she put the abashed Maria through such a catechism, that Christine was horrified. But the good lady evidently was satisfied for she left them playing tennis while she went on her shopping rounds.

For the next fortnight the girls put in at least an hour each morning on the tennis courts and Christine reaped the benefit of Maria's expert coaching. The Swiss girl, on the other hand, talked as much English as possible, and so they helped each other mutually. Christine learned many things about Switzerland and promised that if ever she got the chance, she would visit Maria in later years, and when, in return, she related some details of her own life, she was so soothed by the other girl's comforting words, that she did not notice the astonished look that flitted across Maria's face.

It was fortunate that this new interest had come along, for Christine was being treated practically as an outsider by the two Peters girls, who hitherto had been so friendly. She was still sharing their bedroom, but no longer did they wish to hear of her escapades. They were much more interested in Flo's accounts of life at Greycourt and full of admiration for her "goings on." They were really proud of their sister who was giving them such a good time while she was home, and they were inclined to be on the defensive with Christine on her account. Sometimes though, they included her in their conversation.

"How's your old Swiss?" inquired Dolly one evening. "That's right! Don't answer—you *are* polite!"

Christine, who had been drifting off to sleep, started up. "Oh, I didn't know you were talking to me. She—she's all right. I only play tennis with her, you—know."

"Hm—yes, of course. She's only a servant."

"Now, look here," Christine, thoroughly exasperated, bounced up to a sitting position, "once and for all, I will not have—"

But at this point, Flo knocked on the wall. "Shut up, you kids, and go to sleep," she called out, and though Christine was indignant at being addressed in this manner, she lay down again and closed her eyes. Dolly and Louise whispered together for a time and then dropped off to sleep, but Christine felt, before she followed their example, that she was losing her spirit and self-confidence.

And the next morning, Maria bade her good-bye. "There is great trouble at my house," she explained," and I may have to leave. The master of the house, whom I have never seen, has been

drowned, and I think some disgrace is coming to
them. So I try to cook somesing good for them
and feed them well. I will not come again to
play, but soon you return to school, is it not so?
And you will perhaps write to me?"

"Yes, of course I will," Christine promised,
warmed by the girl's loyalty to her employer in
her time of trouble. "I do hope things will get
easier for them. You write to me."

And they parted—Maria to comfort the be-
reaved family and Christine to become more
lonely than ever. Flo went back to Greycourt,
but the tension in the house did not ease up at
all. Mrs. Peters seemed to be making up for any
holiday slackness by indulging in a perfect orgy
of spring cleaning. Now that Sally was better,
the two girls were out with her all the time,
only returning at bed-time each night. And
when they went back to school, the neighbourhood became unbelievably silent.

"I've got to admit I'll be glad to go back to
Greycourt," Christine said to herself honestly.
"I didn't think it would be like this at all. Thank
goodness it's not much longer to the twenty-
third." She drew a deep breath and made a
resolution. "I'll try to get on with everybody
this term, and even if they won't be friendly
now, I'll work hard anyway. It'll be wonderful,
just being back again."

But the days went on and nothing was said

about her return to Greycourt. Mr. Peters took to his bed with a "nasty cough," and Mrs. Peters seemed more harassed than ever. The days went on until it was nearly the twenty-third, and then it *was* the twenty-third and Christine had not gone back to Greycourt. She fought down a sick feeling of disappointment and tried not to worry Mrs. Peters who was now nursing her husband through an attack of pleurisy. But life definitely was grey for the girl, and she lay during the night of the twenty-third, with the salt tears running unchecked down her cheeks. This was the end of all her hopes and she had no one to thank but herself! Towards morning she fell into a fitful sleep, and woke with a headache. But with the morning her courage came back to her, and she scowled at her reflection in the mirror.

"You coward! Pull yourself together. No use moping now; you'll just have to make the best of it. If Maria can go to Commercial School, so can you. So—chin up!"

Mrs. Peters mercifully was pre-occupied with her sick husband, and the girls had gone to school, so after washing the breakfast dishes, Christine was able to go for a brisk walk. She returned at dinner time feeling better, and listened to the girls as they discussed a new teacher at school.

After Mrs. Peters had packed them off to school again she said to Christine, "Did you want to go out particularly, my dear?"

"No, thanks, unless you'd like me to do any shopping for you."

"You've been very good and a great help to me," Mrs. Peters told her, a smile lighting up her tired eyes. "But I'd be glad if you'd stay in this afternoon in case the doctor comes before I can get back. Then, if he wants anything, you can get it, can't you?"

"Yes, I'll look after everything, Mrs. Peters," promised Christine, glad to have something definite to do and Mrs. Peters went off with her mind at rest. For a time Christine sat reading by the fire. The house was quiet and all the clocks seemed to be ticking extra loudly. But she couldn't concentrate on her story. It would be necessary to make some sort of plan. She wasn't being given a chance to return to Greycourt, but if she made a big effort, her father might still have reason to be proud of her. She bit her trembling lip. Poor daddy! She'd let him down badly; he'd be so disappointed about this. And in spite of her fine resolutions, Christine's head dropped dejectedly on her hands, and she gazed into the fire, with all the spirit gone out of her. Some time later, she heard the key in the front door, and roused herself to greet Mrs. Peters, who she supposed had hurried back in time for the doctor.

But—the kitchen suddenly seemed to brighten, to be filled with the fragrance of fresh flowers and sparkling life, and there, radiant and friendly, stood Dolores Cameron.

"I met Mrs. Peters and she gave me the key," she explained. "I've come along to tell you some news I know you'll be glad to hear."

Christine jumped suddenly to her feet, dropping her book and overturning her chair. "Oh, Mrs. Cameron, don't say it please!" she cried, her eyes bright with tears. "I'll do—I'll do—oh, do let me go back to Greycourt!"

CHAPTER EIGHTEEN

A FRESH START

Dolores was so astonished that for a moment she did not speak. Then she smiled tenderly.

"My dear little girl, of course you are going back to Greycourt. That isn't what I've come to tell you."

Christine, with relief and gratitude welling up within her, raised her tear-lashed eyes. "Father?" she breathed.

"Yes, dear—wonderful news. Your faith in him has been justified and he will be with you soon. Let's sit down, shall we?" And Dolores pretended to be busy settling herself while Christine recovered. The girl herself was glowing with happiness; she felt as if she were coming to life again. She wasn't really taking in the story that Dolores was telling. Her father would soon be free—that was all that mattered. Dimly she heard again the details of the crime for which her father had been tried—negotiable securities lodged in the Bank's strong room—missing— one of the bonds found among her father's private papers. Christine's thoughts went off at a tangent to those weeks of horror; the commitment and trial of her father—her mother's disappearance, for it did not seem possible that she was dead. The strength of circumstantial evidence had made the result of the trial a foregone conclusion, and she had suffered the dreadful shock of hearing that her father was to serve three years' penal servitude for a crime of which she knew in her heart he was innocent. And now—now—

"The ways of life are indeed strange," Dolores was saying, still in that soothing tone, "the man who was responsible was drowned when a collision took place in a fog, and an investigation of his effects revealed the greater part of the missing securities, which he had been using as collateral in his gambling on the Stock Exchange. But you don't want to hear all this do you Christine? You're only glad about your father, aren't you?"

Christine nodded happily. She could not speak.

And then, in came Mrs. Peters and the doctor, and for the next few minutes all was bustle and excitement. But later, when they were sitting down quietly to a cup of tea, Dolores remembered something.

"Christine, what made you think you mightn't be going back to school?"

"Term began on the twenty-third," Christine said.

"But I wrote—"

Mrs. Peters gave a start. "Oh, my, dearie me!" she gasped in dismay, drawing a letter out of her bag. "I put this in here intending to read it as soon as I got a chance, but I've been so bothered this last week I clean forgot it." She opened the letter and read it painstakingly while the others exchanged amused glances.

"In it, I explained that term doesn't commence until the thirtieth, because of repairs and alterations," Dolores said with a whimsical smile. "I also explained that I have been rather off colour or I should have been over to see you. Never mind, we've still got a few days left and we'll do what we can."

With Dolores, as always, to resolve was to act. Before another hour had passed, Christine and all her belongings had been packed into the car and kindly Mrs. Peters was waving them off.

The last few days of the holidays, spent at Dolores' home *were* very enjoyable even though they included visits to the doctor and dentist, and Christine recovered completely her health and spirits. Just before the Greycourt train steamed out, she gave Dolores such a grateful and loving kiss, that that lady's eyes were misty for quite a long time afterwards.

Back at Greycourt, Christine rushed up the

stairs two at a time, eager to see the girls again, but the first girl she met was Hilda.

"Oh dear!" Hilda said querulously, "can't you walk upstairs properly? This is very trying at the beginning of term!" Then she hunched her shoulders defensively, expecting a retort from the Fourth Former.

"I'm sorry Hilda," Christine answered quietly. "I was just excited. I won't do it again."

"Oh—oh—that's all right then." Hilda was very relieved. "I'm glad to see you back," and she hurried off.

Conquering a feeling of shyness, Christine opened the door of the Fourth Common Room and went in. One or two of the girls looked round and smiled, but the majority were too busy talking to hear her entrance.

"Well, brace up, old dear," Ronnee was saying, "we can't expect to have it all our own way. After all, there are several weeks before the match; surely some arrangement can be made. You *would* do something clever like that!"

"Born awkward!" commented Katie Dean grinning. "Some people just are."

Maureen's wrist was lightly held in a sling. She had been helping in a flooded area, and had hurt her wrist rather badly. Now she was down-hearted about not being able to play tennis. Still, there was plenty to do besides and she cheered up.

"Why, hullo, Christine! So, you've come back, after all?" cried Ronnee, noticing the newcomer for the first time.

"Yes, and I was glad to come back," Christine admitted.

"Good for you." Ronnee and the Fourth appreciated her honesty. "It's not such a bad old place. Had a good time? The weather has been so shocking that I don't suppose you have. And now Maureen has had to do her wrist in, just as we'd thought of having a go at the tennis and the literature. We'll have to give them up— we're just unlucky!"

"Chris!" Sheila and Priscilla stood in the doorway for a moment and then rushed over and greeted their friend. Christine, though still shy, was feeling happier than she had done for weeks. She hadn't realised how much she liked the atmosphere of school life, with its fun and badinage and even its troubles, until she thought she was losing it. And now she had something to work for. Her father would come here to see her soon, and she must have something in the Honours way to show him. And she'd start now!

"Er—would you—" she began, but no one listened. Even Sheila was discussing the literature prize.

"It ought to be easy enough," she was saying persuasively, "I don't know about you, but I'm ashamed of that empty shelf. It shouldn't be hard to write one decent essay each, and get all the marks we can for English."

Several looks were directed at Christine. "We *have* tried," Janet said defensively. "We've told you why we've never succeeded. What's the good of putting a spurt on now?"

But Christine intended to start this term right. "It's because of me, I know," she said frankly. "You needn't try to hide it. But I won't—I promise you I won't—put any more spokes in the wheel. You see"—she coloured up but went on bravely, "my—my father is innocent, as I always said, and I'm so happy, I—I—I—"

She bit her lip up and could not go on. But the Fourth wouldn't have let her, anyway. They crowded around, congratulating her and displaying such wild enthusiasm that Christine's heart went out to them in gratitude. She was soon herself again, and told her story to a very sympathetic audience. The tea bell rang as she was finishing, and the girls all scrambled downstairs together, thrilled with the happy ending of Christine's sad little tale.

From that day onwards, everything seemed to change in the Fourth. Christine felt that she had to make up to her form for the way she had let them down previously, and she wanted her father to be proud of her when next they met. So she made prodigious efforts at all subjects, somewhat to the dismay of the Fourth, who had anticipated an easier climb up the hill of recovery.

"You're like Eustace—too bloomin' 'olesale!" complained Ronnee. "What with you and Sheila, we can't call our souls our own!"

It was the same at games. Christine had one purpose, which was to play good tennis. She would play tirelessly, and persuade any one she could find to practise with her. Her games with Maria were bearing fruit, and she was beginning to be known as an outstanding player.

Her path was not entirely smooth these days however, and one afternoon she was made to realise that she still had to live her former reputation down. The whole school wanted to contribute to the Flood Distress Fund, and the music mistress was organising a concert for that purpose. All the forms were to provide some form of entertainment, and in due course, Miss Dyson came to the Fourth.

"Now then girls—here's what I want. The Cockney sketch you did last term—that's for you and the Lower Fifth, and there's a part song for you only. Three of you in the sketch—Sheila, Connie and Janet. Now the song—Ronnee, Maureen, Priscilla, you at the piano, Katie, Alison—no, Christine, not you, dear, Sally, Daisy, Valerie and Dorothy."

It was said kindly, but quite definitely, Miss Dyson had not forgotten the last concert in which Christine had taken part.

"Rehearsals begin to-morrow, and the concert is next week. Neither of the items is new to you, so two or three rehearsals should be sufficient. Three o'clock sharp to-morrow!" And the music mistress left them.

The girls felt rather sorry for Christine but, and she sensed this, a little relieved too. Things were apt to go wrong when Christine was mixed up in them. True, this term so far, was going swimmingly, but it was a little early to be sure.

"We've got time for a game before tea Chris," Sheila put in quickly. "Come and practise that underarm with me." And the two went off together. There was not a free court, however, so they walked and talked of their plans until it was time to go in.

During the next few days, Christine found it hard not to give way to her rising resentment; she had not become a saint overnight, and it was galling to find herself almost the only girl in the Upper Fourth, not taking part in the concert. Still, she managed to keep her temper, and was rewarded. One afternoon, she walked across to the playing fields to watch the Sixth play tennis. There were very few girls, for rehearsals were in progress, but as she watched, the Head Girl came out, racquet in hand.

"Hullo, Christine!" she called out. "Pouf! Isn't it hot! Terribly stuffy at rehearsal. I'm glad my bit's over. Aren't you playing?"

"No, Margaret," Christine said with a smile. "There isn't any one."

"Don't you call me any one?" demanded Margaret in mock indignation. "Get your shoes and racquet quickly and we'll have a game."

"Oh!" Christine was delighted and ran like a hare, to change. Margaret looked after her approvingly—the kid was more amenable this term, probably growing up. I expect this'll be a bit slow," thought Margaret, the crack tennis player, as Christine came running back, "but it will be worth it if it makes her more contented at Greycourt.

But Margaret soon lost her tolerant smile. The game was by no means a slow one, and she only beat the younger girl by a narrow margin. When the game was over, and a pleased and proud Christine had run off to tea, Margaret stood for a moment looking thoughtfully after her.

The concert was given the next week before a crowded and enthusiastic audience, and a generous sum of money was collected for the Lord Mayor's Fund. Mrs. Cameron, who had come for it, sat with Christine during the performance and when she was leaving, whispered something about a box of fruit and cakes. It wasn't long before Christine was sharing these out with the rest of the Fourth, who received them with loud cheers, and they declared them to be the best part of the whole day. The girls were beginning to know and like Christine now that she was more approachable, but although she responded to their advances it was Sheila she sought always—Sheila, who would always have her grateful affection—Sheila, the girl who had befriended her in the face of all opposition.

CHAPTER NINETEEN

THRILLS AND CHILLS

"And what are you so shiny-eyed about?" enquired Sheila coming upon Christine unexpectedly as she ran into the common room for her library book.

It was true. Christine's eyes were like blue stars as she turned, waving two letters at her friend. "Oh, Sheila!" her voice actually lilted with happiness. "Things are coming right all of a sudden! I've heard from Daddy at last— and there's a letter from Maria too, and it's the weirdest thing you ever heard of!"

"Is it?" laughed Sheila. "What on earth are you babbling about?"

"Well, listen. Daddy says—oh!" Christine broke off with a little sigh of excitement, "you can't imagine what it's like to hear from him again—it's nearly as good as having him here."

Sheila smiled but did not speak and Christine went on more calmly. "Well, he's not going back to the Bank ever again. He's going to take over a hotel in Surrey. Won't that be marvellous?

Mrs. Cameron's father arranged it all—isn't she the most wonderful person you ever met—she just can't stop being kind."

"Yes, she's an absolute dear," Sheila agreed, getting a word in. "Why don't you call her Dolores as she asks?"

"Oh, I don't know—perhaps I will one day. But I'm so thrilled about this Surrey place. You know Sheila, at the back of my mind, there's always been a dread of going back to our old house, and I've felt I just couldn't bear it because of all the dreadful things that happened there. But this—this is best of all—"

"Yes, do tell me some more. And you'd better come along while you are telling me or the best books will be gone."

Christine caught up her book, and danced along the corridor with her friend.

"Daddy says he's coming to see me as soon as he is presentable. I think he means he has been ill." She sobered down and began to look thoughtful, and Sheila broke in hastily, "And Maria? What about her?"

Christine brightened up. "Oh, yes. Well, Maria will soon be out of a job, but it's all right, because Mrs. Cam—Dolores, I mean, badly needs help in her London home. And later on, she wants someone to talk languages to little Joan. But *I*'ve got a plan too!"

Sheila giggled. "I bet you have—well?"

"When our hotel is going strong, Maria will come to us. She knows lots about cooking, and she can speak several languages. *And* she can practise English as much as she likes. Isn't it wonderful?"

"I should think it *is* wonderful," Sheila told her as they chose library books.

"Hi, Sheila! Don't forget the literary," called out Katie, the librarian.

"Oh, yes! I'll write, truly."

"And don't forget, you others, Ron, Maureen —use your left hand—Connie, Janet—let's fill up the shelf before we get out of the Fourth."

"And me?" Christine put in, hating to thrust herself forward when she was ignored, but determined to win back an honourable place in the form if she could.

"Of course, if you like," Katie said levelly, but obviously she did not think Christine would contribute anything. "Better look at the rules; they're over there." She pointed over to the notice board.

"All right," Christine said quietly. She went over to the notice board. The notice was in Margaret's clear handwriting.

"Fourth Form Only.

Entries for the Literary Prize must be handed in by Friday, May 23rd. The conditions are as follows:

(1) Subject—Description of a famous char-
    acter of fiction.
(2) It must be your own unaided work.
(3) Not less than 500 words.
Apart from the prize offered, if 60 per cent of
the entries are of a satisfactory standard, a row of
books sufficient to fill the shelf reserved for this
year's Fourth, will be presented to the form."

And then Margaret added her own character-
istic little note.

"Come on, Fourth! Fill up your particular
shelf! It's time you got a move on in the matter.
No Fourth has let the donor down since she
instituted the custom. You're not going to
either, I know! Good luck to you all!"

Christine squared her shoulders. "I'm going
to get that," she said to herself, and from then on,
she added practice in essay-writing to her tennis
practice. As the weather brightened up, classes
were held in the open air as much as possible
and all the girls seemed to be freshening up like
flowers after rain. The Fourth, hardly able to
believe in its "luck," were settling down seriously
to their school tasks and Miss Masterson, their
form mistress, began to lose her harassed look;
it seemed as if her form were making some sort
of headway, after all. Christine, who never

did things by halves, caused some of them to groan at the standard they now had to attain, but they were impelled by her energy to rouse themselves to further efforts, and for several weeks, the Fourth had a very creditable showing when the weekly roll of school honours was read out.

Dolores came along on two occasions and took Christine, Sheila and Priscilla out to tea, and Christine was happy to be with her and always affectionate. It seemed as if everything in her world was sunshine now. Her father wrote regularly once a week at least, sharing all his plans with her and asking her to be patient. But she didn't need that really; she was quite content to do as she was told and try to make up for the fuss and trouble she had caused. She didn't mind being teased now!

"You're much too good to be true these days," Ronnee told her with a grin, one afternoon as they were playing tennis. "Aren't you ever going to break out again?"

"Not if I can help it!" laughed back Christine sending over a smashing ball.

"Ouch! You little wretch! What, not even a teeny-weeny dormy feed?"

"No—not even that. You—you do see Ronnee don't you, that I want to have something to show Daddy when—I see him?"

"Oh, stop protesting. 'Course I see. He'd

probably like you better your old self though," Ronnee couldn't resist saying.

"That wasn't my old self—I say, let's stop talking about me."

"All right with me. Service!" and they went on with their game.

It was not within reason that Christine should work so hard at her tennis and the captain not notice it. Indeed Margaret noticed many things that people with less powers of observation would have missed and she had been called "a red-hot nuisance" by some of the lawbreakers of Greycourt. However, she had been turning matters over in her mind with regard to the forthcoming tennis match between Greycourt and Stonehurst and she had come to a decision.

"Miss Craven," she said to the school tennis coach who was in residence for the summer, "I wish you'd watch Christine Barry and see if she's good enough for a reserve in the Stonehurst match. I know very well you weren't pleased with us yesterday, but I almost believe she could replace one of those lower Fifth reserves. Would you please?"

"Yes, Margaret, I'll try to fit it in," promised Miss Craven, who had known the captain since she had been a junior Greycourtier. "I'll let you know."

Like most busy people, she did manage to fit in another job, and Christine's heart jumped into her mouth when she heard Miss Craven ordering her to go on the tennis court and play. But later Miss Craven's report to Margaret was so favourable that the Fifth reserve girl was dropped and Christine came running in to the Fourth, bubbling over with excitement.

"Oh, girls—I can hardly believe it, but I've been chosen to play—if it's necessary—in the Stonehurst game."

Well, that *was* an honour for the Fourth, and it spoke volumes for the success of her endeavours that no one was envious.

"This'll put the Fourth right on top," crowed Katie, "'specially if we manage the literature as well."

"Yes, don't you dare slacken off, young Christine!" admonished Ronnee. "You've let yourself in for something now and we'll keep you up to it."

"I'll take care of that," she laughed back. "Coming, Sheila?"

And the two chums went off together. They usually liked to walk and talk at least once every day. They always had plenty to tell each other and Christine grew more gentle and happier as her friendship with Sheila progressed. To-day Sheila had an invitation for her.

"Mummy wants you to come home with me for the break at Whitsun," she said.

"Oh, Shee, I *couldn't*," her friend cried, blushing

at the memory of her last holiday at White Gates. "Surely your mother doesn't mean it?"

"She does. Look Chris, dear, you've started again here and done wonders. Surely you're not going to be a coward about a little visit like this? My young sister is always asking about you and Mummy laughed about Christmas the last time I was home. Oh, and you remember George, the boy who made you angry? Well, the last time he was over he said he'd tell you next time he saw you that he'd been an idiot about Bonstead. It's a grand place and he's met a lot of fine people there. So you see?"

"Oh, Sheila," was all Christine could say and they walked quietly for a little while; then Sheila broke the silence. "By the way, you never told me the weird news about Maria."

Christine looked blank for a moment. "Maria? Oh, yes," she remembered. "Maria, of course. Fancy, and it's most frightfully exciting."

"Well?"

"Well, I'd told her something of what happened to Daddy. We'd sort of exchanged confidences, you see. But what neither of us knew was that she was employed in the family of the man who had wronged Daddy. As you know, this man was drowned—poor man—and it was among his private papers or something that they found the proofs of my father's innocence." How proudly she brought that out!

"There was such a to-do in the house that even Maria got to hear of it. She had to help to quieten the lady who wanted to burn all the papers. And when she heard the details they were so like what I had told her, that she grabbed the evidence before the lady could do anything about it. And then she told them what had happened and how my father had been imprisoned and mother had died from the shock. The lady was broken-hearted and wanted amends made at once. You see, Sheila, this lady has plenty of money of her own and she didn't know anything of her husband's business matters. It seems a funny way to go on doesn't it?"

"Very funny," agreed Sheila, who knew about most of the money difficulties at home.

"Even mother, who was as delicate, always asked Daddy if things were all right when he used to come in looking tired. Of course he'd never worry her with any of his troubles."

"Yes, but what about Maria?"

"Oh, yes. Well, she looked after the lady and told her she'd be happy to do whatever she could to lift the burden off her shoulders. But the lady—I don't know her name, and I hope I never hear it—said that she and her daughter would go abroad as soon as they could, though she was grateful to Maria for her kindness in their trouble. So then Maria went to the Welfare Centre to see Mrs. Cameron—beg pardon, Dolores

—but she hadn't been there for some time, so Maria wrote to the address they gave her there. She was afraid to tell me about it herself in case it was too much of a shock! Well, there, I'm out of breath you see. Dolores came tumbling along as soon as she had made sure it was true and I've loved her ever since. Phew! I must sit down."

Sheila dropped down in the seat beside her. "It's the most wonderful story I've ever heard," she said softly. "Three cheers for Maria!"

"Talking of stories," Christine brisked up, "I'll have to send in my essay by Friday. I *do* hope—oh, I've left my racquet—"

"Where?"

"It must have been in Margaret's room. She sent for me just as I was coming off the court and I went along just as I was. In my excitement I forgot it. Had I better leave it now?"

"No, I think you'd better collect it. Margaret won't want her room cluttered up with racquets. Go along now—you've got time."

"All right. I'll come along to prep afterwards." And smoothing her hair Christine hurried along to the head girl's room. She paused to get her breath back at the top of the stairs and then became aware of a girl's voice raised angrily. She noticed that the head girl's door was slightly open and was about to turn away, when, instead, her feet seemed rooted to the ground.

"You may be the head girl, Margaret, but you've no right to put that little prison person in the game. It's not fair. It's disgraceful to turn me out for her. I'll make such a—"

"Marjorie!" came the head girl's voice sharply, but the Fifth Former went on recklessly, "I don't care, I will say it. Her father's been in prison and it casts a slur on the school. It's like a smear across the tennis court and all the girls in the game will hate it. If you do play her I'll call her Jailbird, or something like that, in front of the other team. You won't remove me without regretting it I can assure you."

But, here, Christine ran down the stairs as quickly as she could. Out through the open door she ran not knowing where she was going, and she made blindly for the tree near the domestic quarters, where she'd been accustomed in earlier days to hide from the rest of the school. Still, in a blind panic, she climbed up into its leafy branches, and clung there panting and trembling.

"Well," came a mocking voice from below, and there was Flo, looking up with an amused twist in her mouth. "I thought you'd reformed?"

"Don't—don't give me away please," Christine managed to whisper through her quivering lips. "Please don't."

The smile left Flo's face. She was not really an ill-natured girl, and she could see that Christine was distraught.

"Don't worry," she whispered back reassuringly. "Stay there till you feel better. No one will see you." And she went back to the kitchen.

Christine sat for a long time in the old tree, thinking. Her head ached and her heart ached too. It was no good, she told herself, no good. Best thing she could do was to leave Greycourt. But, oh! Jailbird! If anybody ever said that to her in private she'd feel badly enough, but if it were said publicly, as Marjorie had threatened, why then, she'd want the earth to open and swallow her. And then what about Greycourt? Perhaps after all it was better this way. Greycourt was really too grand an old place to have —what was it?—a smear across the tennis court. "I can't do much to add to its fame," she thought, "but at least, I can prevent discredit falling on it," which showed how far she had travelled in the past few weeks.

Fired with high resolves, Christine slid down to earth again and almost fell on Margaret, who was carrying her racquet which had caused the trouble.

"Good gracious!" gasped Margaret, jumping back, "what on earth are you doing?"

"I'm sorry, Margaret," was all she could say.

"Here's your racquet. And take fifty lines for being here at all, let alone climbing about in that stupid fashion. I did hope for better things from you Christine."

No response from the girl except that her head dropped a little lower.

"Well, all right. Don't take it too much to heart," Margaret said patting her on the shoulder. "You needn't do the lines till after tennis on Saturday."

Christine mumbled something.

"*What* did you say?" Margaret gasped.

"I—I—I—thank you very much, Margaret, but I'd rather not play."

But instead of the outburst that Christine had expected and dreaded, she felt Margaret's hand gently drawing her on to the seat below the tree.

"Any one been upsetting you?" asked the head-girl quietly.

No answer.

"Tell me please," insisted Margaret. "I intend to know."

"I—I just think it's better for me not to, that's all, Margaret."

"Tut-tut! Shocking grammar! And why do you suddenly feel this way? Did you—oh, my hat!" exclaimed Margaret suddenly and with no thought to her dignity. "Were you coming up to my room for this," pointing to the racquet, "when you heard that rigmarole? Yes, I know you were; you needn't try to deny it. Up you get—quickly and come along with me."

Feeling rather scared by now, Christine accompanied Margaret to her room.

"Now then," that lady said cheerily, "make yourself at home for a few minutes and have this." She poured out a glassful of grapefruit squash and put three biscuits in a saucer. "Mind you've finished them up by the time I get back."

For want of something to do, rather than because she was hungry, Christine drank the grapefruit and nibbled the biscuits and she had just finished them when the door opened. But when she saw who was coming Christine jumped nervously to her feet.

"It's all right," Marjorie Wellard said with a sheepish grin. "Now don't go getting all of a doodah or I'll be in hot water again. No, wait, let me say my piece. Margaret tells me you heard what I said this afternoon. I'm sorry about that—really I am. I was only furious because I'd been kicked out and—well you must admit you've been a bit of a nuisance in your time; it didn't seem fair that you should take my place. But evidently you left before the real speeches came. You didn't hear Margaret's little address?"

"No—no, I didn't." To her own amazement Christine felt she was about to smile, and that surely was not appropriate to the occasion.

"Well, she started off by telling me that Grey-court was founded for the children of poor Christian gentlemen and that each succeeding generation had tried to keep the accent on the Christian part. Then she asked me if I'd like to leave the place. And I said: 'No, of course. Who wants to leave old Greycourt?' Then she said that nobody else wanted to leave Greycourt either, but that if I did what I threatened to do, you'd want to leave. She also said she was sure I wouldn't want to stay if I thought I'd driven another girl out. Well, considering I'd said all that in a temper, and had forgotten what I'd said, I thought she was being a bit grim, but," Marjorie shrugged, "you know Margaret. Anyway Christine, it's a great pity you heard it all, though you must have eavesdropped a bit, mustn't you? Don't see why you shouldn't have some of the blame. I *didn't* mean any of it and I *do* hope you get a chance to play. If you do, remember I shall expect you to do your utmost, because that's what I'd have been doing if you weren't a little bit better than I am. Stonehurst are marvellous players—we'll have a job to beat them. All right now?" she asked grinning.

"Oh, thank you, Marjorie." Christine just couldn't help laughing for sheer relief. "I promise you I'll play my hardest for your sake, if I have to play."

"Good-oh. Go to it and don't let me down."

Christine "went to it" harder than ever after that with the result that her essay, which she had rewritten several times, was handed in promptly on the Friday and she was keyed up to fighting pitch for the match on Saturday.

CHAPTER TWENTY

HAPPY BIRTHDAY

The weather was so unfavourable at the beginning of the day that it looked as if Saturday's big event would have to be abandoned. But, after a dull morning with rainy gusts of wind, the weather changed, and the sun shone out in a cloudless blue sky, for the match. Although it was so early in the season the school looked forward to the series of games held on this particular Saturday, for there was a long standing rivalry between the two schools. Actually Stonehurst had carried off the palm more frequently in former days, but since an official coach had been installed at Greycourt much more attention had been given to games, and this afternoon they were hoping at least to hold their own with Stonehurst.

The Sixth and Fifth formers all looked fighting fit, and it seemed very unlikely that Christine would be called upon to play. She was rather relieved on the whole, for since she had been practising with the prospective players, with big Jane Bishop, and that terribly quick Anne Molyneux, and Margaret, she was convinced that she was not up to their standard. So she settled down quite contentedly to watch the brilliant game and set which followed. Greycourt won the first round—could hardly help it, with Margaret playing so superbly, thought Christine. They lost the next, and the next, and the Greycourtiers' hopes began to fade. But perhaps the set-back was just what was needed, for Greycourt went in again with grim determination and won the next round by sheer hard hitting.

And now it was the turn of the fair-haired captain of Stonehurst to rally her girls, but somehow, their enthusiasm had been dampened and their Fifth Form opponents had a fairly easy task in beating them. The Stonehurst captain was regretting by this time that she had not sent her best player in before this, but Greycourt had been easy to beat in former years. However she sent her in to give a brilliant finish at least, to the afternoon's show.

It was at this point, that Hilda Cartip, sitting on a bench with Jane Bishop, who already had played, suddenly spied two juniors straying into the forbidden precincts of the tournament field. She sprang up so suddenly that she upset the bench and tipped Jane on to the row of Greycourt girls just behind. They all leaned forward to assist the toppling Jane, and over went their own bench. A shriek of mirth arose from the crowd of them and even the Stone-hursters stood still to laugh with them, for they certainly presented a comical sight. It wasn't until they were all sorted out and fairly composed again, that Margaret noticed that Anne looked a trifle wishy-washy.

"You all right, Anne?" she asked anxiously.

Anne jumped to her feet. "Yes, thanks," came her assurance promptly—too promptly, for she immediately sat down again, flinching.

"Oh, you're hurt, poor old girl!" Margaret cried.

"No, I'm not," the other girl said obstinately. "Don't fuss, Margaret. I'll be all right in a minute, you'll see. It was only the old bench toppling on me."

But here Miss Craven came hurrying up. "Let's see," she said soothingly, running her fingers lightly over Anne's foot. "Um, you'll be all right I think, but you're not going to play to-day, my child."

"Oh, Miss Craven!"

"That's enough, dear, you must trust my judgment. Margaret, will you choose a reserve for this round?"

Margaret looked at her two reserves—a Fifth Former who was leaning in a relaxed attitude against the fence and looking a little bored at the whole proceedings, and then at Christine, keyed-up and alert, and ready for anything.

Margaret made her decision.

The Fourth Former jumped like a shot when she heard her name, but after the first moment of terror she found reassurance in Margaret's friendly eyes. The head girl walked over to the net with her.

"Just think you are practising, as you were all last week," she said, in her quiet voice. "Eye on ball, and give all you've got. You'll be all right. Good luck!"

Christine murmured an answer to the Stonehurst girl's greeting and then the last game of the afternoon was being played. Christine had very little idea as to how the game was progressing. She only knew that she must keep her eye on the ball and that she *must* send it back accurately. Now and again, she heard cheering, but did not connect it with herself. She was concerned solely with sending that ball where it belonged, and she would have continued to do that till she dropped if it had been necessary. When it was her "service" Maria's coaching stood her in good stead, and her balls went just over the net with deadly precision. And then, just as she realised that the game was coming to an end, there was a commotion, and the Stonehurst girl was running up to the net, holding out her hand. Christine, in a dream, shook hands and murmured her thanks, and then Margaret and the rest of the players were upon her, patting her on the back, clapping, and generally making such a tremendous fuss over her that she was overwhelmed.

"You were wonderful," Anne said generously. "I couldn't possibly have done better."

"I'm pleased with you," was all that Margaret said, but she said it in a way that made the Fourth Former glow with gratitude.

"Thank you, Margaret," she said hurriedly. "May I go now?"

"Go? Where? Oh, I suppose you want to see your friends. Just one minute then—well, perhaps five—and then come back and have tea with the visitors."

"Oh, Margaret!" was all Christine could gasp, as she ran off to her waiting form.

"I don't believe the kid knows she saved the situation for us," laughed Margaret to the others. "My word, she's got a smashing service."

She had already congratulated the Stonehurst girls on their fine game and had received their congratulations in return, and they all now made their way into the school together.

Of course Christine was the heroine of the hour, as far as the Fourth were concerned. The sight of her on the field, forgetting self, and playing with all her might for the school, had at last melted their distrust. Every grievance they had ever had against her, every annoyance she had ever caused them, were forgotten. With one accord they took her into their midst again, and this time she had the sense to stay there and not repeat her former mistakes.

After that wonderful afternoon, and the still more wonderful party given for the visitors, Christine settled down again to the Fourth Form routine, but now, she looked forward hopefully all the time and her face generally was alight with anticipation.

The Whitsun break came, and, a little apprehensively, she went home with Sheila, who was delighted at the change in the girl whom she had befriended. Mrs. Conway had acceded to her daughter's appeal only because the holiday was so short and she did not like to disappoint her children, but she was glad now that she had given the invitation. Christine caused no trouble during this holiday which sped by quickly and pleasantly.

She made her peace with George, who, after approaching her rather fearfully, found to his relief, that she was 'a smashing girl' and went around singing her praises. But Julie, Sheila's younger sister, was frankly disappointed.

"Oh, dear! You're not half the fun you used to be," she complained. "You're just as prim as old Sheila. Don't get like her, whatever you do."

But the other two just smiled at each other, and refused to be drawn into an argument.

"Well, anyway," persisted Julie, curling herself up in conversational fashion on the sofa, "tell us what you'll do when you see your father."

"Oh, I've thought of several things," Christine told her, with a flash of her old arrogance. "I'll show him any prizes I may have won and any weekly "honours" (I've got one already), but I'm going to tell him that henceforth I intend to devote my life to making him happy, and I shall say, too, that my one aim will be to make him forget the dreadful past."

The other two were duly impressed, though Sheila looked slightly puzzled.

And then the holiday was over and they were back at Greycourt for the summer term, which, they noted, "flew by faster than any term they'd ever known."

On the Monday after they came back, the winner of the Fourth Literature Prize was announced. "There was some difficulty in choosing here," Miss Meredith told them, with satisfaction gleaming in her eyes. "The final choice lay between Connie and Christine, but it was decided that Christine must have revised and rewritten hers several times because the article had a "polished" appearance. So, Christine Barry, my heartiest congratulations to you on your splendid work—you are a credit to your form."

After the vigorous clapping had died down,

Miss Meredith continued, "As the general standard was satisfactory your vacant shelf is to be
filled with books of your own choice, so you may
each write down the name of a book and let me
have it. I am proud of my Fourth Form," she
concluded with a friendly smile, and she descended
from her rostrum. It was evident that the Fourth
was quite proud of itself too, though its members
tried not to look too self-conscious. And so the
"happy term" flowed along.

In the meantime, Sheila, Priscilla and Christine
spent a great deal of time out of doors, getting
to know the country, and getting to know each
other and at intervals putting in vigorous games
practice. There was no question of the Fourth
showing up badly at the end of this term. The
same force of character which had caused Christine to make herself such a nuisance formerly
now propelled her and her form-mates along in
the right direction.

"I can quite see old Chris captain of Greycourt,
can't you?" Sheila remarked one day to Priscilla.

"Easily, my dear," her friend replied. "She's
only got to want a thing badly enough, and she'll
move the earth and us on it to get it. I rather
think that's why she was up against Mrs.
Cameron so much. They're very alike you know."

"Why, so they are! You're a clever old thing."

"Elementary, my dear Watson! Look, I've
got this for to-morrow."

"This," was a beautiful set of brushes with mirror. For to-morrow was Christine's birthday.

"Lovely! Mine's coming in the morning. Cake from Mother—beads from Julie—gloves from the boys—yes, they each gave a coupon— some marvellous fruit from George—he thinks Chris is a 'stunner' now! And I'm giving her flowers and a nice little brooch that Mother's managed to get. I hope she'll be happy—I do hope so."

"Well, she ought to be with all that."

And Christine certainly was! Her birthday was full of happy surprises for her. First all the girls sang "Happy Birthday" to her in the Common Room after lunch, and crowded around to inspect her presents. Then Mrs. Cameron had sent a most wonderful hamper for a birthday feast as well as a fountain pen and a propelling pencil. And among her birthday post was a tiny note from her father which pleased her most of all. It said: "Wanting so much to see you, dear, it won't be long now." She had that note in her pocket and kept patting it.

"I'm thrilled with everything," she murmured. "You're all such grand sports."

"Oh, you're not so bad yourself, Chris, now we know you," Ronnee told her graciously. "Don't mind our calling you Chris?"

"Oh, no, I prefer it."

So "Chris" she was from then onwards. But

that wasn't all that happened on that wonderful
birthday. For, as the Fourth sat ploughing
steadily through the birthday tea, Margaret
came up and whispered something in Christine's
ear. The girls saw her flush up and then go
pale—and then, she smiled radiantly around at
them and disappeared.

"Girls, it's her father!" exclaimed Sheila.
"I'm absolutely sure of it."

So was Christine. She sped along to the
Common Room—picked up her Literary prize,
one or two small "honours" she had won and her
presents and hurried along to Miss Meredith's
room. She was telling herself to be sensible and
calm, and rehearsed in her mind the little speeches
she had prepared, to say to her father.

But—when she got at last into the Headmistress' room and saw the gaunt, wistfully
smiling man who awaited her, she forgot her
speeches and with a great cry of longing and
of love, ran swiftly into his outstretched arms.